DREAMS OF MOLLY

Dreams
of
Molly

a novel

Jonathan
Baumbach

DZANC
BOOKS

1334 Woodbourne Street
Westland, MI 48186
www.dzancbooks.org

Published 2011 by Dzanc Books
Book design by Steven Seighman

06 07 08 09 10 11 5 4 3 2 1
First edition April 2011
ISBN-13: 978-0982797532

Printed in the United States of America

I am here without wife or woman, your guide and reporter, a hostage to the habits of rerunning the dead past in the cause of waking from the dream.

When Molly left, everything burned. I was vulnerable to the touch of air.

—*RERUNS*

PART ONE

(Dreams of Molly)

35th Night

It was not the same. It was all the same. I was in Italy sitting at my desk in a luxuriant Villa writing the story of my invented life. I was in bed in Brooklyn dreaming I was in Italy at the Villa Mondare, which was a made-up place in any event, writing the first sentence of a fictional memoir. My wife, who was no longer my wife, who had left me years ago for greener pastures, was in the bathroom dyeing her hair (back to its original dirty blond) so that I would remember with regret what she looked like when I let her get away. I kept asking her if she was done to which she would say, "Any minute now," but hours passed without her emergence. After awhile, my impatience dissipated. I reinvested my concentration on the first sentence of my new book, a sentence so important in the scheme of things, it produced near-unbearable anxiety just to be in its presence, a sentence that, if it were doing its job, which was to segue between the distant past and the relatively near past, would probably need to resist conclusion indefinitely. I heard the toilet flush in a secretive manner as if evidence were being destroyed. "Is everything all right in there?" I asked. "I'll be out before you know it," she said.

I had always been impatient. Everyone who knew me knew I had a history of impatience. Anecdotes abounded, whispered exaggerations. As soon as I started a piece of writing—story, novel, memoir, poem, shopping list—I felt driven to complete the job. I wanted to be where I was going the moment I conceived of taking the trip. And yet more often than not the trip itself, the daily skirmishes with the page, had its own grudgingly acknowledged pleasures.

I returned to my chore. (Was she coming out of the bathroom anytime soon or not?) The sentence I was contending with stalled.

Plagued by distraction, I wondered if all of the scholars at the Villa Mondare had a former wife (or mate) in the private bathroom adjoining their accommodations. There was something in the brochure, which I had glanced at in passing, about providing each scholar with everything he would need to complete his project. Was Molly, if that's actually who it was in the bathroom—I had not seen her yet—intended as a kind of recovered muse? I decided to ask her when the time was right how she happened to be in my bathroom at the Villa Mondare.

"If you went away for thirty minutes," she called through the closed door, "I'll be out when you get back."

"Why can't I just stay here," I said.

"You know why," she said, "and don't pretend you don't. It's virtually impossible to get anything done when you know someone impatient is standing at the door waiting for you."

I retreated from the door and returned to my desk, working silently on my recalcitrant sentence, adding a word here and there while barely touching the keys of the selectric typewriter I had been issued. Then it struck me that Molly would know I was still there because she hadn't heard the outside door slam closed.

So I tiptoed to the door, opened it carefully and closed it with enough noise to wake the building.

"Are you back already, Jack?" she called through the door. "That's so like you. It's not thirty minutes yet."

So I left my room, joined my shadow self, on a time consuming walk, returning thirty-one minutes after Molly's original request. The night had been quiet and uneventful except for the painter in residence painting from nature in the apparent dark. We exchanged grunts when I passed her.

"Time's up," I said to Molly.

"I'll come out," she said, "but you'll be sorry. What I'm doing takes longer than anyone knows."

"I'm willing to be sorry," I said.

And still there was no sign of her.

"If you promise to look the other way," she said, "I'll come out."

"I'm turning around," I said, hoping to sneak a glimpse over my shoulder.

It was only after I turned all the way, that I heard the bathroom door open. "When can I look?" I asked.

"You can turn around when I tell you to," she said. "Deal?"

I nodded my agreement, used the time standing with my back to her trying to remember what she looked like that fateful day fifteen years ago when she announced it was over between us... No image offered itself.

"What happens, Molly, if I turn around?" I asked, eager to see her even with the unattractive plastic bonnet over her hair.

I meant to keep my part of the bargain, but the extended silence intensified my curiosity. I sensed her shadow moving stealthily in the direction of the bed.

I turned my head warily, barely an inch, then turned back quickly, catching a glimpse of red dress as evanescent as a flash bulb explosion.

Perhaps I'd seen nothing, but my expectations, minimal in the best of seasons, glowed with promise.

36th Night

In the morning she was gone. I had actually written the line in nuanced anticipation an hour before she left. "Do you remember me?" she asked. She was sitting on a stool on the other side of the room, her face in shadow. I leaned forward, strained my neck to get a better view. She offered me a right profile, removed her plastic cap, shook out her hair.

"Of course," I said. To be honest, I was not absolutely sure.

"Could you come a little closer."

"If you know me, you'd know me anywhere," she said. "Anyway, I'm feeling a little shy."

The wall switch controlling the overhead light was behind me and to the left. I reached back over my shoulder, hoping to flip the switch before she was aware it was happening. I tried unsuccessfully to turn my head and keep her in sight at the same time.

"What are you doing?" she asked. "Why is your hand behind your head like that?"

The voice struck a chord or perhaps it was what she said. Though embarrassed at being found out, I didn't dissemble. "I was looking for the light switch," I said, returning my hand to my side.

"That's so sneaky," she said. "The terms of my residence in your quarters—read the small print in your contract—is to be in the shadows of the room during working hours. If you turn the ugly overhead on, I'll have to leave. Is that what you have in mind?"

I had nothing in mind beyond determining whether she was the real Molly. The voice was passingly familiar, though it lacked authoritative context or perhaps I had willed the voice's more or less familiarity. "What happens after working hours?" I asked.

The question seemed to trouble her and she offered me the back of her head in exchange. I repeated the question or the question repeated itself and I got the same answer, which was no answer at all.

"It was good of you to visit," I said, which produced a muted sardonic laugh.

Eventually, I left the room to go to lunch (or was it dinner?). Eventually, I came back from dinner with two dinner rolls wrapped in a napkin for my temporarily disappeared guest. Eventually, I re-read my opening sentence in progress, which ran two pages without conclusion. Which seemed to have lost a few words in my absence, a sentence with no memory of its past and with fading hope of a future. Eventually, I accepted the fact that she was gone from the shadows of my magisterial room. Eventually, I felt abandoned so I gave up my unresolved sentence to search the grounds.

While I was gone, I worried about finding my way back, which produced paralyzing anxieties. Circumstantially, I found myself behind the avant garde visual artist working at her easel in the unyielding dark.

"Getting what you want?" I asked.

"Yes," she said, "and go away."

"You didn't happen to notice a woman perhaps wearing a plastic cap over her hair go by?"

"Someone went by about an hour ago," she said, "but it was too dark to see who it was and besides I was working, which let me remind you I still am."

I spent the rest of the night in the hallway of the Villa in the vicinity of my room, no longer sure which door was mine, trying to remember the first words of my sentence.

I must have entered the nearest door because when I woke up at first light I was in an unfamiliar bed in a room much like my own though conspicuously different.

I knew the room wasn't mine because the pieces of under-clothing dangling over the odd pieces of furniture strewn about were female apparel.

I thought it might be fun to write in a room that had an erotic subtext though I worried that the prospect of real sex might become distracting.

Moments after I locked the door someone knocked and I left the bed to answer it, realizing on the way that I had nothing on but a t-shirt that extended six inches below the knee. The clothes I had been wearing—my writerly outfit of workshirt and jeans—were nowhere in evidence.

I thought whoever had been there had gone away while I was looking for my pants, but momentarily the knocks returned with renewed persistence.

"Come back in ten minutes," I said to the intruder behind the door, hoping to be fully clothed when whoever it was claiming my sanctuary returned to displace me.

37th Night

Hours passed without further incident. After awhile my my circumstantial quarters achieved the status of long-term familiarity. Molly had a late afternoon cameo in my borrowed bathroom only to disappear again as a way of gaining my attention.

It couldn't be said that she was always missing. It was that she tended to be absent when I longed most to have her around. I told her as much but she remained skeptical or indifferent. She kept redyeing her hair, never getting it quite the right shade of dirty blond and so almost always in the bathroom when I needed to use it. I tended to pee on the grounds in the dark, noted by the visual artist who kept her own counsel, while perhaps including me in her black-on-black nightscape.

As much as I liked being at the Villa, as much as it seemed the best home I'd ever known, I knew I couldn't stay there forever.

I had lost my letter of instructions but memory reported that I had three or four more days allotted me. The unfamiliar case I found in a corner of the room already packed with odds and ends in anticipation of my eventual eviction.

When I asked Molly if she was staying on to be the muse of the resident coming in to replace me, she said, "Funny, I thought it was you who was supposed to be my muse. Does this look like a man's room to you?"

I couldn't say that it did without lying inexcusably.

That's what happens, I suppose, when you find yourself occupying a room with women's clothes strewn about—you lose your sense of place in the world.

So I went out into the hall to look for my old room, knocked on a few doors. Various residents I knew only from a distance answered my knocks, invited me in for a drink or not, seemed at home with themselves.

There were two more doors left to investigate and I approached the first one warily in the hope of discovering a more productive strategy, my fist in the air withheld from the door.

The door abruptly opened and I was confronted by a woman dressed in black, who I imagined I recognized as the painter of nightscapes. "Yes," she said, "this is or was your room, but as you can see I'm here now."

I wondered out loud why they hadn't given her her own room when she arrived.

She stepped aside to let me go by. "They did sort of," she said, "but then one day I discovered someone else had taken it when I was out doing my art so I commandeered the first unoccupied room I could find. We could share it if you have no other place. I tend to sleep during the day and work at night so we shouldn't get in each other's way."

I looked at my watch. It was on the cusp of nighttime, and she would be leaving in an hour, she said, to do her work.

Everything else in the room, I noticed, was mine except for three black canvasses prominently displayed, two on the wall, one alongside the wall opposite the bed.

I accepted her offer and went back to my sentence as soon as she left the room. It was a little different from how I remembered it, but also less hopeless, more susceptible to ultimate resolution.

38th Night

The painter-in-residence didn't return at first light as promised and I had my room to myself in a sense. The black paintings on the wall had a way of insisting on their presence in a disconcerting sometimes oppressive way. They were signed—at least the two on the wall were—with the initial Q. The one on the floor, which I assumed was unfinished, had the signature letter roughed in, near invisibly in pencil. Odd, I thought since the painter's name, the name she introduced herself to me by, was Leonora.

If she ever returned, I would have to remember to ask Leonora what the Q stood for.

When I wasn't writing—by this time I had moved on to the second sentence—I wondered if it were a coincidence that the two women in my life had both disappeared. Then it struck me that going back in time all the women I had ever known, starting with my mother, had eventually deserted me.

Feeling abandoned, I left the room in search of company.

When I returned the paintings were gone, at least no longer on the wall and I assumed—what else could it mean?—that Q (or L) removed them so that she would no longer have a reason to return.

But that night, someone shook me from sleep, wanting to know what I had done with her paintings. It was Q (aka Leonora) and she had paint on her hands which transferred to the shoulder she had shaken.

I protested my innocence and then went off with her on a prolonged and seemingly hopeless search for the missing black paintings. A sense of responsibility will take you down odd paths.

We went from room to room on tiptoes, looking in closets and under beds, taking something from each of the rooms in compensation for the loss.

We had quite a haul of stuff in an orange garbage bag when we returned to our room to discover Q's black paintings on the walls again—all three this time—returned by the thief in our absence.

Q was pleased, though not greatly pleased, hugged me, and then began to moan, complaining that whoever took the paintings decided they weren't worth keeping, which was hurtful and cruel.

"Perhaps the slanting of the light had blinded us to their presence before," I said.

I meant only to console her, but it led to something else, something more or less, and we were on the floor together irrevocably entangled when, after a staggering knock on the door, some official entered (the Assistant Director in charge of Transgressions—she wore a button to that effect) to banish us from the Villa. From my vantage on the floor, the angular young woman, who bore Molly a passing resemblance, seemed bigger than life.

39th Night

Q (or L) and I left the Villa together in disgrace and relative poverty, forced by circumstances to wander from one look-alike town to another, doing whatever came along to earn our keep.

With the last of our lira, we bought some realistic-looking imitation metal chains and I improvised a strong man act in the various town squares. Q (or L) would tie the chains around my chest and I would huff and puff and groan until it seemed I had given up and then I would break my bonds by seemingly expanding my chest. The unit had a trick link that came apart when yanked on in a certain way. Each time I gave the illusion of breaking my bonds, Q would scream with pleasure as if she had never seen anything like it before.

I would shrug at her amazement while Q collected money from the crowd in one of her hats and arranged portrait commissions at half price with some of the locals. The money we earned was better than nothing, though not a lot better.

Q suggested we collect the money before the show, but that didn't seem sporting.

For the most part, we slept out of doors or in somebody's barn, using the others' proximity to keep warm.

We kept our spirits up by makings plans to return to the Villa under different identities, but of course we knew it was just idle talk. They warned us on leaving that we could never return no matter what we did to redeem ourselves, no matter how much time passed.

In the early days on the road, Q and I seemed pretty much of one mind about everything. But after awhile, we began to squabble about where to go and what to do and how to spend the little money we had between us. After one of our fights, I took the sock with the money and left Q in the deserted ramshackle barn we had been using as residence.

Four or five drinks later, when I returned to our temporary residence, she was gone and her small suitcase with her. She had left me one of her paintings—the blackest of the nightscapes, the one I professed to admire—as a parting gift.

I didn't miss her for the first few hours of our separation, wrote an abbreviated version of our tragic love story in the ratty notebook I'd been carrying with me.

The last line was: "He expected to miss her after awhile, after a week or so, but as it turned out the expectation sufficed for the feeling itself."

When the story was finished, when the last line that had been playing through my head got itself down on paper, I couldn't imagine how I would get on another day without her.

40th Night

You could see it was an all day rain, but since I was low on funds, I went on to the next village with the idea of doing my strong man performance in the town square. As usual, particularly since I started drinking again, I was short of cash.

I put up signs in the usual places, but when the time came to begin, there was no one in the audience. Eventually, a carbinieri showed up carrying one of my signs and waving it at me as if it were a weapon.

I assumed he was ordering me to leave and I packed up my chains, but on the contrary he was insisting that I perform for him even though he was the only spectator..

He had a folding chair and an umbrella and he opened them both and made himself comfortable.

I tied the chains rather awkwardly—it was generally Q's job to tie the supposedly unbreakable knot—while the carbinieri watched intently.

I went through the motions of failing, which was part of the act and my audience laughed and clapped his hands. "He can't do it," he said to no one in particular.

His skepticism provoked me. I took a deep breath and expanded my chest, expecting the chains to come apart as they always did.

I panicked at first when nothing happened, but then I thought I hadn't tried hard enough. So I took a deeper breath, expanding my chest to the breaking point, but the chains resisted me. It then struck me that these were not the chains I had been using. Someone, no friend of mine, had made the switch.

* * *

The small crowd in attendance—I hadn't noticed them as-semble—started throwing things, fruit for the most part. There was also the occasional puh-ching of flying lead and I fled the stage, leaving my equipment behind.

I ran without looking back until, several miles down the road, I tripped on a loose sixteenth century cobblestone and I fell in a sprawl by the side of the road. The passing thought that held sway was, Whatever else happens, Jack, you can't get much lower than this.

41st Night

I ran into Q (or L) again at the airport in Milan. She seemed to have forgotten that we had separated on bad terms and gave me a hug and told how she had made all this money selling paintings, some of them commissioned portraits, to Americans returning home. She only needed twenty-one more dollars to afford her own ticket back to the states. On the other hand I was sixty-nine dollars short. My Visa card, which I assumed was good, was rejected repeatedly.

It was almost like old times. Q had a set of chains in her carry-on bag and after a couple of drinks of red-eye for courage I performed for the captive crowd on the tarmac, a glass window separating us.

That I still had it or had regained what I had lost or was drunk enough not to notice how tacky my act was improved my shaky self-esteem.

We made a killing, though most of the bills Q collected in her hat were in unrecognizable foreign currency.

The exchange booth was closed so we had to live in the airport for a while, plying our respective trades.

To get rid of us, the authorities put us on a plane going back to the states but because of weather or perhaps faulty navigation we ended up in Newfoundland for refueling purposes.

We made the mistake of getting off the plane with the others during what they told us would be a seventy minute stopover. But as we had no tickets, when we tried to reboard the plane, the woman at the gate denied us entry.

When Q argued, they arrested her, and when I protested her arrest, they arrested me and though we had American passports, after a week's imprisonment in a makeshift cage adjoining the food preparation room in the local MacDonald's, they deported us back to Italy.

The Italian authorities refused to accept us—there was a fraud charge on the books against us—and we found ourselves once again on a plane going back to the states.

We fought continually on the plane ride back, and by the time we reached Boston—the destination of this particular flight—we were no longer on speaking terms.

Q's passport had expired during the delay and under duress I had left mine in Newfoundland so we were detained together, as it turned out, while the authorities reviewed our situation.

I made an effort to be polite, though it was unfelt, while Q (or L)—they addressed her as Leonora—remain sulkily tight-lipped.

They searched our luggage for clues. My chains were seized as undetermined evidence against me. Two bottles of pills were commandeered from Leonora's case as well as one of her lesser nightscapes.

While we were detained, we couldn't help but overhear the following conversation.

"I'm for going by the book but it's not clear to me how the book reads on this case," said official one. "You know what I'm saying?"

"I've seen the new regulations—you're going to love them when you see them, lots more freedom of initiative, they just ask for creativity—though they don't actually go into effect until 3:00 this afternoon."

"Bummer. What time do you have?"

"We could always push the clock ahead if we have to, if time in this case is of the essence."

"For argument's sake, let's say time is of the essence."

While this conversation was going on in the next room, Leonora and I shared the occasional desperate glance. We were sitting next to each other at this point, our hands meeting as if inadvertently on the bench between us. The guards were talking in whispers now and it became increasingly difficult to pick up more than an idle word.

"We're in this together, whatever it is," she said, "and I'm not going to be afraid."

Momentarily, the door opened and one of the guards entered the room. "I need to use the facilities," I said.

"Use whatever facilities you like," he said. "You're free to go." He unlocked the door behind us and held it open, standing absolutely still while awaiting our departure.

We were standing now but made no attempt to leave. Leonora asked the guard to repeat what he said.

"It only gets said once," he said. "That's the regulation."

I took Leonora's hand and tried to lead her through the door and she took a step or two then stopped at the doorway, refusing the final step to freedom, glancing at the guard, who had not moved since he opened the door for us, who was standing at attention with an almost imperceptible smile, a congested smirk on his inexpressive face.

42nd Night

We separated at the revolving doors, exchanged phone numbers and shared a gypsy cab into the city. The otherwise silent driver was the first to notice. "There's been a pink Cadillac following us for the past three miles," he said. "I'll try to lose him for you if that's what you want."

I studied the Cadillac through the back window, recognized one of the airport security people as the driver. "Lose him," I said.

"Whatever," Leonora said.

The driver, who had an eastern European name with no recognizable vowels, warmed to his task. He got off the highway, indicating his destination at the last possible moment, made a series of sudden haphazard turns, throwing us together in the back seat in compelling ways. The next jolt separated us, but the following intricate maneuver brought us together even more persuasively.

We rode at dangerous speeds through back alleys, jumped a fence or two, crashed our way through the back wall of a garage, damaged a few unwary parked cars. If I wasn't inescapably tangled with Leonora and my hands were not otherwise occupied, I would have applauded the performance.

When the dust cleared, our oversized pursuer was still in the driver's rear view mirror.

"There must be more than one of them," he said, "or this guy is top of the line."

It was a glum realization and we each in turn bemoaned our lot.

"We'll pretend he doesn't exist," I said. "It's worked for me before. Just drop us at the nearest motel." I was intent at taking to its conclusion what circumstance had set in motion.

"I finish what I start," the driver said, "or my name isn't whatever it says my name is."

I started to protest but Leonara deflected my argument with a kiss.

So we drove awhile on back roads with a sense of purpose that made us feel we were getting somewhere. After a while, the driver admitted ruefully and with some reluctance to our being hopelessly lost.

It was Leonora's suggestion, but the driver took it up immediately as his own. "Why don't we just follow the pink Cadillac," she said.

"They seem to know where we're going."

Once we got ourselves behind the Cadillac, discovering its two occupants in heated dispute, our former pursuer seemed to have no problem accepting its new role. It led us the grimmest possible version of a merry chase. Eventually, we found ourselves on the highway going against the traffic. Survival seemed a low percentage option.

The more it tried to lose us with cunning maneuvers, the more determined our driver became to hang on its tail.

Eventually, it pulled up in front of my former house (or a similar house on a much too similar street) and we took the parking space two doors down.

We hunkered down in the cab waiting for the people in the pink Cadillac to make the first move. They seemed to be waiting for us to do the same.

Our driver, exhausted from his exertions, had fallen asleep, was snoring as if it were a jazz riff.

And, so caught in the grip of our long standing circumstantial passion—actually it was a reconnection this time— Leonora and I spent our first night back in the city, waiting for someone else to make the first move.

43rd Night

In the morning the pink Cadillac was gone, taking with it our most persistent topic of conversation. We didn't have sufficient cash to pay off the cabdriver, who had run up a huge tab on the meter, so Leonora stayed in the cab as hostage to our debt as I warily approached my former residence.

It was no great surprise that the lock refused to entertain my key so I leaned on the buzzer.

A man I knew slightly in other circumstances answered the door. "I hope you're not selling anything," he said and then he recognized me and closed the door in my face.

I leaned on the buzzer with renewed persistence.

The same man answered, a woman who bore Molly an uncanny resemblance standing behind him with her arms crossed in front of her.

"What in God's name do you want?" he asked.

"I want to know what's going on," I said. "I used to live in this house. The woman standing behind you used to be my wife."

"And?"

I had no answer to the question of And so we faced each other angrily, perhaps uncomprehendingly, without benefit of language. "Look," I said, which was everything I had to say.

"If there is nothing else," he said and would have closed the door in my face yet again if I hadn't gotten my foot in the requisite space.

There was something else, something lucidly inchoate that I was unable to imagine into words.

"Darling, I'll phone the police," said the familiar voice behind him.

"I don't think that will be necessary, sweetheart," he said, and I had to restrain myself from thanking him.

Leonora, who had worked her way to the bottom step of the stoop, climbed up alongside me. I sensed some kind of belligerent energy coming off her, which set off a distant alarm.

"You might be a little more civilized about this, you prick," she said, her arm puckered in the air like a cat's paw.

"I'd ask you in," Molly said, "but the place is an unholy mess."

"Nothing can be gained from this," my replacement, Donald, said, once again locking my foot in the vice of the door. The woman who resembled Molly disappeared briefly, returning with an over-sized shopping bag which she thrust in my direction between the man's arm and his side.

"This is probably what you came for," Donald said in Molly's voice. Perhaps he was lip-synching for her. I was too close to the scene to make an exact determination.

When I reached for the bag, the hand extending it withdrew. "You have to move your foot first," someone said.

"Don't be a sucker," Leonora said, which made everyone laugh.

After that, after the shared laugh, the tone of things changed and we were invited inside to see the improvements they had made in my exile.

"I was hoping to see an unholy mess," Leonora whispered in my ear. "You know, I'm beginning to like these people."

As we toured the house, which seemed pretty much as I remembered it, we were invited into the kitchen for coffee.

Donald, who seemed to be wearing one of my old jackets, asked if he could interview me for his new book, which dealt, as far as I could understand his explanation, with the sexual behavior of the recently divorced.

I said no, said it twice by my count, but as Molly later reported, Donald's success in life had been dependent on never taking no for an answer.

Molly muttered something to Leonora and they were gone before I had actually seen them leave.

"Shall we begin," Donald said, straddling the chair opposite mine. He riffled through the pages of a notebook before settling on a question. "How often did you pleasure yourself during the first month of your separation from your former mate?" Donald asked, reading the question from a notebook.

It was none of his business but I could see telling him that was not anacceptable response. "I don't remember exactly," I said.

"More than ten times?" he asked.

I went through the motions of thinking about it. "Well…" I said.

"More than fifteen? More than twenty?"

"It's possible," I said.

"I'll take that for a yes," he said, writing something down that seemed longer than the word Yes. "How many times did you have sex with another person during that first month?"

"One," I confessed, stretching the truth.

"What was the gender of your partner?"

"What?"

"Man or woman?"

"Woman."

"Was she younger than your former wife or older?"

"I don't know… Younger, I suppose."

He smiled inappropriately. "Was this someone you had met when you were still living with your wife?"

"I'd rather not answer that," I said, perhaps unnecessarily wary.

"I'll take that as a Yes," he said.

"If you do," I said, "you could well be making a mistake."

"This kind of fencing is not much use to either of us," he said. "I promise you that your name will not appear with your answers. My assumption is that if you hadn't met this partner before you and Molly separated, you would have no problem telling me that."

We got no further with the interview. Without announcing themselves first, the women reappeared.

"How's it going?" Leonora asked. "Getting a lot of good stuff?"

"We'll probably need another twenty to thirty minutes," Donald said.

"Don't be such a stick, Donald," Molly said, giving him a light kick in the leg. "Jake looks all talked out to me. Besides he's never been able to tell the truth for more than fifteen minutes on end." Leonora laughed on cue while Donald studied his notes.

Odd, I thought, she had never called me Jake before. Was this the wrong house? Was she the wrong former wife?

44ᵗʰ Night

Donald never finished the interview with me, but said when I reminded him that he had used his God-given gift for empathy to fill in the remaining answers for me. I was planning to ask him if he had done the same with other subjects as well—the man had no shortage of overweening confidence—but I never got the chance since he and Leonora disappeared together the next day.

"Hey, it's like déjà vu," I said to Molly, referring to our being alone together, but she was not so easily consoled, and at the same time locked in denial.

"He always comes back," she said, "dragging his tail behind him."

I didn't know what she meant. "Are you saying that he's done this before?" I asked.

"Never," she said, "though he tends to be absent-minded and sometimes loses his way." She giggled at a memory that excluded me. "You know, it could be circumstantial that Donald and your floosie are missing at the same time. What's your opinion?"

"Could be they both lost their way," I said.

"When we were this official couple," she said, "you were never this supportive. It seems to me you've matured since our break-up." She offered me her hand for safekeeping.

Later, after a dinner of left-overs, which seemed fitting, sitting close to me on our old couch, she mentioned that she happened to glance at Donald's notes from his interview with me and she had a question of her own she wanted to ask.

I knew no good would come of it, though I pretended I had no objection to being asked another question.

"Okay," she said. "This other partner of female gender you mention, okay, this so-called younger person, was she on the scene before we were smart enough to separate?"

I saw no point in hesitating. "No," I said

She laughed and pointed a finger at me. "That's not what you told Donald. There's no reason anymore not to tell the truth I'd appreciate it as an old friend—tell me the truth just this once."

I could not remember what I told Donald nor was I sure what the truth was, the combination making me uneasy. I told the only truth I knew. "I don't like being interrogated," I said.

"Is that because lying makes you uncomfortable?" she asked.

After our first five intermittently blissful years together, Molly tended to put the most unflattering interpretations to the motives for my behavior. It didn't help that she was at times (not that I ever admitted it) disconcertingly on the mark. It's hard to live with someone so relentlessly intuitive. Eventually I confessed the worst, usually through the evasions of denial.

Caught up in nostalgia, I said to her, "When I was living with you, you were the only woman I ever loved."

"Liar," she said, and turned her face away so I wouldn't notice that she was almost crying. I could tell that she wanted to throw something at me and I left the room to save her from her worst instincts.

45th Night

When Donald wasn't interviewing for his sex book, he gave private classes in Self-Confidence and Public Speaking to corporate executives on the rise. In the interest of continuity and contributing to the upkeep of the house, Molly suggested that I take on Donald's students until the prodigal managed his return.

I let it be known that self-confidence and public speaking were not areas of my expertise, but Molly said in the larger context that hardly mattered. She said self-confidence should be everyone's expertise and she gave me a book Donald had written on the subject called, "You Are The Best You Even If You Don't Know It," which I found difficult to penetrate though I read almost every word, dozing from time to time but managing to get the pages turned. I had a sense of accomplishment when I finished the book, let myself believe I was ready to take on whatever came my way.

I had taught some over the years, but I had never imagined myself teaching Donald's subject.

I tried different approaches. With my first client, a shy stutterer in his early thirties, who had inherited his hated father's business, I did most of the talking, invented an expertise for my character that of course had no basis outside of the imagination's presumption. After listening to twenty minutes or so of my inspirational prattle, the client got up from his chair and walked to the door.

"Is there a problem?" I asked.

"Please," he said, speaking with more fluency than he had when he came in. "You sound just like my father." I suppose I knew what he meant. In any event, I had been so full of myself during my encouraging talk, his walking out on me was a crushing blow.

I took the opposite tack with my next client, kept silent through most of the session while the man, a baby-faced hotshot executive still in his twenties, famous for his mercurial rise in the movie business, recited his shortcomings. At the end of the hour, he asked me my opinion on what he had been saying.

Having mostly tuned out through most of his tiresome recitation, I said that I mostly agreed with his assessment.

"Then why does everyone else in the world think I'm so great?" he said with unexpected belligerence.

"I can't imagine," I said.

"I get what you're doing, man," he said. "It's brilliant, man, but I hate that kind of low-rent psychology. Totally hate it. I don't have to take shit from anyone, man, and that includes you." He was a small man but he stood in front of me, stood over me, with his fists balled. "When I feel this way, I want to kick someone's ass."

I played the hand dealt me. "Aces, man," I said. "That's precisely the response we were looking for."

Later, after super-brat left, prancing out on the balls of his feet, I reported to Molly that I was getting the hang of the self-confidence racket.

"I was listening in," she said, "and let me be the first to tell you, you have a long way to go to fill Donald's shoes."

When she said that, I realized that I was at the time actually wearing a pair of Donald's shoes, which aside from pinching the small toe on my right foot, were a near perfect fit. "I'm open to pointers," I said grudgingly.

"You have to be tougher with them," she said. "Let them know who's calling the plays."

I let her remark echo in my head, listening for murmurs of irony, but I heard none. "Is that right?" I said, a further prodding.

She continued in her sternest manner. "I'll assume that's a rhetorical question," she said. "Didn't you read Donald's book? You have to teach by example, Jake, show them from the way you handle yourself the virtues of self-confidence."

"Fuck off," I roared at her.

Eventually, when she returned to the den after her composure had been restored, her tears dried, she said with unmediated dislike, "Well, maybe you're not as hopeless as I thought."

For a flickering moment, my confidence soared off the charts.

And so I made my long delayed move, which led to a hectic chase around the apartment, chairs and tables flying in our wake, everything that had been together coming apart, questions and answers, unexpressed feelings, pages of a long discarded uncompleted manuscript.

46th Night

And then one morning Molly went to the drugstore for some unspecified items and didn't return. Confident to the point of insentience, I waited three days without undue concern, with barely diminishing expectation, expecting her to walk through the door at any moment.

On the fourth day, I accepted the possibility that she might not be coming back.

On the fifth day, with a sense of urgency, I gave up the house to search for her, armed with the only head shot of her I could find. It was the bruised photo that lived in my wallet and was, by unreliable estimation, thirty years out of date.

When I showed the photo to our local druggist—we actually had two local druggists—he said he couldn't be sure and that he was a man made uncomfortable by uncertainties.

"I'm looking for an older version of this woman," I said.

"I understand," he said, "but as students of aging have discovered, no two people grow older in exactly the same way."

I had never known him before to be so exacting. "Did you see anyone like her?" I asked. "Anyone remotely resembling her?"

"Oh that's a different question altogether," he said. "If it comes to that, I've probably seen a lot of women like her."

I couldn't imagine what he meant, but I persisted in my questioning. "Did a woman resembling her come in three days ago at about this time of day?"

When I handed him the photo again, he glanced at it briefly and then slipped it into a drawer under the counter.

"It's not impossible," he mumbled, and turned to a woman who had just come in with a prescription to be filled.

"If you don't mind, I'd like the picture back," I said and then repeated in a louder voice when he continued to ignore me. And then repeated again.

Under the guise of waiting on his other customer, he pretended that I was invisible and without voice.

I found that intolerable.

My patience as always on short leash, I stepped behind the counter to reclaim the photo of Molly which, stuffed into an over-subscribed drawer, had attached itself to a random condom. While I was trying to detach the condom, a storewide alarm went off.

The blast of sound unnerved me. The photo with the condom hanging from it like an appendage held delicately between thumb and forefinger, I ran from the store.

I noted a police car coming down the street and I ducked into a phone booth, where I hung out in a debilitating crouch until two cops emerged from the police car, completed their business in the drug store and drove off. During this extended period, I worked at liberating the condom from the photo with limited success.

When I entered the second and larger of the two local drug-stores, there was a cop already there, browsing among the mouth washes. I couldn't turn around and leave without attracting the wrong kind of attention.

I picked up a package of aspirin and then in another aisle a nail clipper from a low shelf only to discover the oversized cop standing behind and above me. "I use my teeth," he said.

It took a moment for the context to fill itself in. "That's very funny," I said.

"Of all the opportunities out there for a man of my size," he said, "there were only two that attracted me, police officer or late night TV host."

"And which did you choose?" I asked, the question escaping the restraints of better judgment.

His eyes turned mean. "Didn't your mother ever tell you," he whispered, "never to get sassy with a man carrying a gun?"

"It was meant as a joke," I said. "Like you, I also wanted to be a stand-up comic."

"You'd never make it with that joke." He had his hand now on the butt of his gun, seemed unappeased. "You're not the condom thief, are you, there's an all points alarm out for, eh?"

I looked at him in disbelief, wondered if I could make it out the door before he could unholster his weapon.

"Are you the perp who goes from pharmacy to pharmacy, stealing party hats?" he asked. "Have I got your number, Jack, or what?"

"Not at all," I said with the over-earnest conviction of a poor liar.

"Don't get so worked up," he said, cackling. "I was just pulling your middle leg. I had assumed, stupid me, that you knew the drill." He took something off a shelf—a box of condoms perhaps—and stuffed whatever it was in his jacket pocket and made a hasty exit.

A woman working the checkout, no one I'd ever seen, before beckoned in my direction, and it took awhile for me to realize that it was me she was requesting. "Are you the guy looking for his wife?" she whispered to me when I approached.

"She's no longer my wife," I said, "but yes."

"I thought you were the one," she said, shielding her mouth with her hand. "Two men came in just as she was paying her bill and she went off with them. I don't believe... It didn't look to me like she wanted..."

When she stopped in mid-sentence, I realized that someone who disapproved of this conversation was standing behind me.

It was the owner of the store, the pharmacist Dr. Andsons. "Is there a problem?" he asked.

"What do you mean by problem?" I said, taking the crumpled photo out of my pocket, the condom still hanging to it by a thread. "Have you seen this woman in the last few days?" I asked.

"Who wants to know?" he said, looking everywhere but at the picture itself. "I'll tell you this, I may have seen that rubber in its prior life. If I didn't sell the nasty things, I wouldn't allow them in the store. What's the condom got to do with the woman, as if I couldn't guess?"

"Forget the condom," I said. "There's only a circumstantial connection."

"That's a line that's made the rounds."

I held one edge of the picture while he held the other, studying the photo with an almost frightening intensity. "This is my picture," he said. He tried to kiss it but the condom got in his way and he drew his head back in disgust. "This woman, Alma, disappeared from my life twenty-five years ago. What's your connection to this, Bo."

"This woman has nothing to do with you," I said. "This is a picture of Molly, my former wife Molly. She left the house three days ago to go to the drugstore and I haven't seen her since."

"She never liked the name Alma," he said, still clutching his corner of the photo. "She thought it too arty-farty. It was her one fault. So that may explain the change of name, okay? Whatever she chooses to call herself, I still miss her. Hell, I'd take her back in a nanosecond." He tugged on the photo and came away with the attached condom half of it. His elegiac moment was replaced by self-righteous anger. "I'll give you thirty seconds to get your keester out of here before I call the police," he said, and started counting. I let twenty seconds elapse before making my exit.

My half-picture in hand, I went back to the house, hoping someone might have returned in my absence, Molly in particular, though I had long since given up being absolute. I would have settled with reasonable contentment for anyone.

47th Night

Anticipation tends to defeat itself. The house was empty on my return but there was a letter concerning Molly waiting for me in the vestibule. It was poorly spelled, mostly ungrammatical and eccentricly punctuated, though its intent was undeniable. The gist of it was, that if I wanted to see Molly again alive and unharmed, it would cost me a hundred thousand dollars in small bills.

This was their sale price, they said, a bargain considering the value of the hostage. They would contact me again (reported a postscript) concerning arrangements for the transfer of the money.

One hundred thousand was a lot to ask for a woman who was no longer my wife. When I looked closely, I noticed the letter was actually addressed to Donald. I gave a sigh of relief until it struck me that in Donald's protracted absence—he had not left a contact number or forwarding address—the burden of Molly's safety was in my impoverished hands.

To the best of my memory, I had eight-hundred-twelve dollars and thirty seven cents in my checking account and another two-hundred in one of my socks so if I was going to ransom Molly, I needed to raise ninety-nine thousand or so in short order however it might be done. I tried to be systematic, which had never been my strong suit. There was little chance I could raise that much without resorting to crime and I played out that scenario briefly before rejecting it absolutely. Borrowing seemed the last and least fraught of my limited options, and I wondered if I had any rich friends I hadn't thought about for a while.

Pacing the hallway, wandering the various empty rooms of the house, accruing desperation like moss, I had a brainstorm. ninety-nine thousand would seem like chump change to Molly's business exec father. So I phoned Buck, who I wasn't even sure was still alive from an old number which yielded another and then another. He was in a hospital somewhere in California, a woman with a husky voice told me, and was not expected to return home. He was in the cryogenics ward, though no irrevocable decisions about his future had yet been made.

I took down the hospital number, and knowing it was a long-shot, expecting nothing, I got Buck on the phone at first try. "Good to hear from you," he said, though he had no idea who I was. "How much is this going to cost me?"

I laughed, though I knew he wasn't joking. "The money is not for me," I said. "It's for Molly, your daughter Molly."

There was a prolonged silence at the other end.

"Are you there, Buck? I'm calling about Molly."

"Whatever she may have told you about me, it's all lies," he said.

"It's not about what you did. She's being held for ransom by kidnappers."

"She's just a child," he said. "If you showed yourself in person, old as I am and sick as I am, I'd break you in half. You hear me?"

I explained that I was the one trying to get her released, but he persisted in confusing me with the kidnappers.

"How much would you take to let my little girl go free?" he asked in a bullying voice.

"Buck, I want her free as much as you do," I said. "The kidnappers are asking a hundred thousand dollars."

"Would you take fifty?" he asked. "Fifty is a very generous offer."

"Anything you'd be willing to give would help," I said, "but to get her released I have to raise one-hundred-thousand."

"Get a real job, you bum," he said. "I'm willing to pay forty. Take it or leave it. And I want her back all in one piece. You haven't removed any parts, have you? I want everything put back in its original place or we have no deal."

At this point, someone, a nurse perhaps, took the phone and asked me to identify myself. I said I was a former son-in-law calling about his daughter.

"I can't allow you to upset him," she said. "If you told me what you wanted, perhaps I could present the news to him in a way that would disturb him less."

I wasn't prepared to discuss the issue of Molly's ransom with someone I'd never met. "It's a personal matter," I said. "It's also urgent."

"Is it?" she said. "I'll give you two minutes to tell me what this is about and then I'm hanging up. Is that clear?"

I lost about forty seconds reviewing my alternatives and then I told her as succinctly as possible the problem I faced. She laughed when I finished my story.

"You're barking up the wrong tree," she said. "I hope that's the appropriate phrase. I'm here to tell you that Henry no longer has any money in his own name. It was all..."

"Henry?" I said, interrupting her. "I was led to believe the man I was talking to was my former father-in-law, Buck."

"Oh no," she said. "Henry has been given Buck's bed. Of course we changed the linen. Buck was frozen two days ago."

48th Night

Waiting for the kidnappers to get in touch again, I emptied my bank account into small bills. I got a call the next night and a muffled barely audible voice asked if I had gotten the money together. "Not all of it," I said, which was a major understatement.

I could almost hear the mental machinery grinding on the other side of the line. Finally, whoever it was said, "Maybe you don't want your wife back in one piece. Maybe you don't want to see the little woman ever again."

"When we split up—the truth is, she dumped me—I used to feel exactly that way," I said.

"We might be able to take a little less," the muffled voice said, "but then we can't guarantee the condition you'll get her back in. How much you got?"

I was embarrassed to tell him. I wasn't always this broke. It was alimony payments on several fronts that had reduced me to my present circumstances.

"Can you come up with seventy-five?" the voice asked.

When I hesitated, he said, "What about seventy. You can put together seventy, cowboy, huh?"

"I'm afraid not," I said.

"We're not doing a fire sale here? Tell me what you're willing to spend, cowboy, and I'll tell you whether we can make a deal."

I mentioned the money I had taken from the bank and what it combined to when added to the money I had stashed in a sock.

"No way," the voice said. "Just setting up the operation cost us twice that amount. Do you think we're in business to lose money?"

"Look, I sympathize with your position," I said, "but the thousand is all the money I have in the world at the moment."

"If that's your story," the voice said, "—is that your story, cowboy—then all I can tell you is that you'll never see your former wife again." He hung up the phone, or we were cut off from another source, before I had opportunity to announce my regrets.

For the next hour or so, I was at loose ends, envisioning Molly's desperate situation while regretting my inability to save her. I remember her saying years back, right before she asked me to leave, that she couldn't trust her life to me. I had denied it with as much conviction as I could work up on a moment's notice and she had said, "Time will tell."

I was almost prepared to acknowledge that Molly had been right when a knock on the door followed by a ringing of the doorbell, followed by the click of a key in the lock, distracted me from my thoughts.

It figured that the intruder was one of the kidnappers, who had gotten the key to the house from Molly's purse. I looked around for a weapon and, finding nothing that answered to the moment, I settled for Donald's bowling ball which was nestling among his shoes at the back of a closet. It seemed a particularly heavy ball but I lodged my fingers in it and I was swinging it laboriously back and forth to familiarize my muscles with its heft.

I could tell from the sound of running water that the intruder was in the downstairs bathroom, washing hands or peeing or perhaps even taking a shower.

I tiptoed my way down and waited impatiently for whoever it was to emerge, the bowling ball in readiness behind my back.

The phone rang and it felt as if the sirens were calling to me, but just when I decided to leave my post it stopped. Momentarily, the ringing resumed.

Molly came out of the bathroom, unaware of my presence behind the door, and headed for the kitchen phone. "You're safe," I said unable to control my astonishment, the bowling ball slipping from my fingers with a terrifying bang, turning Molly's head.

"You scared me," she said. "Is that Donald's ball that's rolling across the floor? He doesn't even allow me to touch it."

I ignored her complaint. "How did you get away?" I asked.

"You don't even have the right to ask," she said. "Why don't you just get out of here, okay?"

When I said that I would leave as soon as I could get my stuff together, she seemed almost disappointed. "There's no rush," she said. "In any event, I'm going to be away for the next two weeks. The kidnappers are waiting for me in the car. We're going to this adorable island off the coast of Maine."

"No," I said.

"Don't worry so much, Jack," she said. "It's going to be all right." She came over and gave me a quick hug as if someone who disapproved might be watching.

"I'll call the police," I said, which was a concession on my part—I never called the police. "You don't have to go with them."

"When they elected not to kill me," she said, "I felt this sudden surging affection for them. They're not such bad guys when you get to know them. Sweetheart, I'll be back before you know it. Promise."

I stepped out of her way and she was gone.

49th Night

Of course I should have found out where Molly was going—what island off the coast of Maine—before I decided to rent a car and go after her. But then I thought, not having another opportunity to ask, how many "adorable" islands could there be in that part of the world? And then, already caught up in what seemed an urgent agenda, I never should have stopped for the sexy hitchhiker, for which I plead loneliness and boredom.

She had a baby face—she was likely older than she looked—and there was something appealingly (even appallingly) shy about her.

Once I had stopped for her and she had eased her way into the seat next to me, tossing her backpack in the back, there was no way of undoing my impulsive decision.

I made small talk, asked her how long she had been waiting and where she had been going.

She neither answered nor looked in my direction, seemed to be focused on whatever lay ahead.

There was something odd about her, though I couldn't pinpoint what it was. Stopped for a light, glancing at her, I asked again where she was going.

"Wherever this bus goes," she said, emphasizing each word, a sly almost eerie smile punctuating the remark and then disappearing almost instantly.

She was wearing dark glasses and carrying a canelike stick which folded up into something not much larger than a pencil. If she was blind, which was my first impression, how did she see to get into the car?

"I'm going to Maine," I said—we were still in New Hampshire at the time—"and I'll be driving along the coast. So…"

When you're riding in a car with a silent person, there is a temptation to fill the void. I told her about the first time I had been to Maine and the story branched off into areas I had not intended to enter.

She said, "Uh huh," at approximately five minute intervals. At some point, when my story was losing its impetus, she said, in a way that made it hard for me to know that I had heard what I thought I had, "Would you be interested in a little fun?"

I knew what she meant and yet I couldn't believe that she meant it. I suddenly noticed that we were getting low on gas—the fuel sign was flashing—but from the look of things we were miles away from the nearest station.

A few miles down the road a Mobil station appeared in the distance but it disappeared like a mirage as soon as I approached.

And after that, a Gulf and an Arco offered themselves only to disappear before I could reach them. There was even a local brand—Ouija Gas—that was similarly evanescent.

The next time I looked over at my companion, there was a small gun in her lap. "Take the next left," she said. "Don't make me ask twice."

"Look," I said, "I need to find a gas station in the next few minutes or we're not going anywhere." I pointed out the flashing light.

"You should have been more careful," she said. "What kind of father are you?"

"Who said I was a father? Who have you been talking to?"

She lifted the gun and kissed the barrel in a provocative way.

Another Ouija station appeared and I headed toward it, quixotically hopeful as always, the car beginning to cough and fart in desperation.

This time the station didn't fade into smoke as I approached it and I had a moment of elation but then the motor died and I was stranded approximately seven feet from the nearest pump. I sat in the car with my head in my hands.

"I might have known," my companion said, in her expressionless voice. "Nothing you do ever comes to anything."

"I need you to help me push the car," I said.

"I don't do pushing," she said, slipping the gun inside her pants.

Just as I was getting out of the car, three burly men I hadn't seen before came over and offered to help. They got behind the car while I worked the steering wheel, but their first series of pushes, accompanied by ear-piercing grunts, were to no effect.

I realized that I had forgotten to release the emergency break and I waved a hand in apology.

As I released the break, the car shot forward and when it finally skidded to a stop we were as much past the second pump as we had been behind the first one before.

One of my helpers approached the driver-side window and said they had done what they could and now had to get back to their other business. I said that one more push from the other side might do the trick.

"Sorry, cowboy," he said. "There's only one person in town who gets off on pushing from the front and he's gone to his reward."

I noticed that one of the other burly guys was talking to my passenger and she got out of the car and followed him into the convenience store that adjoined the pumps.

Relieved of her weight, the car rolled backwards a foot or so, barely improving my position. I got out, opened my gas tank (which had an awful smell) and stretched the gas pump hose to its limit. Straining the hose a few inches further, I could just about reach my tank with the point of the nozzle.

As I was filling up in this awkward manner, I was distracted by the unlikely sound of a car backfiring inside the convenience store. How odd, I thought.

When it finally struck me what the series of explosive sounds signified, my passenger had returned and we were on the road again, looking for the left turn I had missed the last time around, a smoking gun lying heedlessly in her lap.

50th Night

It isn't that all motel rooms look alike. Or perhaps it is. I speak or demur from limited experience. In any event, when we entered Unit 13 at the Hope's End Motel in single file, my last concern was the general demeanor of the room I was entering at gun point.

My companion, who still hadn't removed her dark glasses, wanted an offspring, or so she intimated, and had chosen me (by default perhaps) to be its father.

Why me? I wanted to ask, but I could see the question had no meaningful answer in present context. Like the motel, I was there.

I sensed that as soon as the transaction was completed, she would kill me so it was in my best interest—my only interest—to stall for as long as possible.

I suggested we first tell each other something about ourselves to take the edge off our strangeness.

"You no longer seem strange to me," she said.

"Strange may not be exactly what I mean," I said. "I need to feel sympathetic to the woman I'm with before I can perform."

"Really?" she said, sticking a hand in my pants to test my claim.

"We need to tell each other our stories first," I said. "Tell me something about yourself. For starters, what's your name?"

She seemed perplexed by my question, her otherwise perfect forehead furrowed. "You can call me Mary. I don't remember how I got here. I've tried to remember but I can't. I don't want to know anything about you so why should you want to know anything about me. You wouldn't believe my story if I told it to you."

"What else?"

"Every man wants to fuck me, that's my story," she said.

It's hard to explain, given that my life was at risk, but her innocence moved me. "I know you don't lie," I said. "I'll believe what you tell me."

"I'm not from here," she said.

It took me a few minutes to take in what she meant by "here" and by the time I figured it out we were already doing the dance.

To be fair, to put the best possible light on it, she fucked like an extra-terrestrial, which was something of a turn-off.

As I later learned, she was a hybrid, part ET, part humanoid, a scientific experiment gone awry. She was interested in others only in so far as they served her basic needs, which were survival and reproduction.

Mary had a particularly long, reptilian tongue and when we kissed open-mouthed it actually did reach down my throat, an odd not quite comfortable sensation.

I resisted climax, which made her impatient, told her I had meds in the glove compartment of the car that enhanced sexual performance.

"How do I know you'll return?" she asked, riding me at some revved-up speed.

I measured my words, my life most likely in the balance. "I want you to have my child," I dissembled. "I sense a sweetness in you, Mary, that you've never been fully in touch with."

"I don't know what you mean," she said, seeming to blush under the glare of the overhead light. "You can go to the car for your meds, as you call them, but if you don't come back, I'll follow you to the ends of the cosmos. Wherever you try to hide, I'll be waiting for you." A reptilian claw extended from her finger and she left a scratch mark under my eye.

I had no doubt she meant her threat. I put on my coat, leaving my neatly folded clothes on one of the matching dressers as hostage to my return.

Waiting for me at the car were a scientific team composed of three men and two women dressed in green hospital scrubs and armed with flame throwers. The apparent leader of the group showed me a blurred photo of Mary, which I reluctantly identified.

"She's already killed five men," he said.

I wasn't surprised, not much. "She doesn't seem so bad when you get to know her," I said.

They asked me to wait around so that I might identify the remains after they completed their "intervention," as they called it. I couldn't bear to watch and I got into my car as the scientists made their way with calculated stealth toward our cabin.

Except it wasn't our cabin they were moving toward but the identical one to the right. I had already started up the car and, though I didn't want to look, watched them out of the side of my eye.

As they were torching the wrong cabin, burning it to the ground, Mary slipped out the door disguised as a man. I was the only one who noticed her.

Wearing my clothes, looking straight ahead, she headed nonchalantly toward the car. I had barely a moment to decide, rush off or wait for her to occupy the space next to me. For whatever reason, perhaps inertia, perhaps misguided sympathy, I didn't leave her behind.

As we drove off, I noticed through the rear view mirror the owner of the motel emerge, bearing what seemed like an army surplus submachine gun. The scientists, searching through the rubble for Mary's remains, seemed oblivious to the approaching danger.

51st Night

"I would say thank you," she said as we sped off into the moon-less night—the sound of fire engines in the distance—"but it's not in my nature to feel grateful."

"That you can say that," I said, "is a hopeful sign. That you are aware of certain positive qualities you lack suggests that these qualities exist in you in embryonic form." She laughed or almost laughed. "Don't bet your life on it," she said.

As we drove across the Maine border, I told Mary of the purpose of the trip, which was to rescue my former wife, Molly, from her kidnappers or, at the very least, from herself.

"When you rescue her, if you rescue her, what happens then?" she asked.

"Well," I said, "I don't really know."

She inhaled my answer, seemingly amused by it. Then, after a few minutes of silent calculation, she offered me a deal. She would help me rescue Molly if we stopped at a motel first to complete our business.

"Is it in your nature to keep your word?" I asked.

"I've never given my word before," she said, "so I don't really know." When she put her hand on my knee, I remembered that I was naked under my coat.

"Why don't we rescue Molly first and then go to a motel," I said, trying to edge away from the demands of her hand. "You can ask anyone. I always honor my agreements."

"You think you're trustworthy," she said in this prescient voice, "but you're not."

A silent compromise was reached through no agreement on my part. Mary climbed onto my lap and attached herself. It made driving difficult especially when she bounced up and down obstructing my view and I began to swerve out of my lane.

When I could see the road again a steroidal SUV was coming at me and I had to bail out to avoid a fatal collision.

What I didn't notice was the tree coming at me from the other side. I heard Mary's unearthly scream before I blacked out.

I woke in what turned out to be a hospital bed, my head swathed in bandages, my left leg in traction.

The scientists I had met at the motel, four out of the original five, were standing impatiently at the side of the bed waiting to talk to me.

There were none of the bedside amenities one gets from most hospital visitors, no "how are you feeling", no "what can we get you." "Did you climax in her?" was what they wanted to know.

The thing is, I couldn't remember but I saw no point in getting them upset. "I don't think so," I said. "Where is she?"

"We thought you might be able to tell us," their spokesman, the bald Asian said. "There was no sign of the ET when we found you. Did she say anything about where she might be going?"

We went back and forth in this manner for awhile, each of us assuming that the other was holding back information.

"We'll find her," they said on leaving, though their insistence was not encouraging. Each of them left me a card with a different phone number.

It was at that point that I realized that the nurse who had been standing to the side during the fruitless interview with the scientists was disconcertingly familiar.

There actually seemed like two nurses for awhile—the bang on my head had given me double vision—but as she came closer I could tell there was only one of her.

"Don't worry, I no longer want your child," she said, disconnecting my left leg from its traction device.

For an unexamined moment, I suffered feelings of rejection. Mary had cut her hair and dyed it black and somehow changed the shape of her nose. "You told me it was your life purpose to reproduce," I said.

"That was another me," she said. "I've changed since the accident separated us. I've been what you people call reborn. I took refuge in the Church of Laundered Money and I had a spiritual conversion. As my first good deed, maybe my second, I'm going to unite you with your former wife."

I took pains to explain—most subtleties were beyond her alien comprehension. "I don't want to unite with Molly," I said. "I just want to rescue her from her kidnappers."

"Whatever," she said.

Before I could make sense of the implications of Mary's conversion, she had gotten me dressed and was wheeling me down the halls of the hospital and out the back door to an oversized SUV (perhaps the one that almost hit us) waiting for us in the medical personnel parking lot in a space reserved for Hospital Chaplain.

Whatever else you wanted to say about my semi-alien companion, she had a cunning way of getting by the authorities.

52nd Night

Before we could continue our search for Molly, Mary felt honor-bound to return some items she had taken by force from a convenience store during her heartless pre-conversion period.

What she didn't realize was that it was more dangerous to return stolen goods than to acquire them in the first place. Also, which no one had told her (and she probably wouldn't have believed anyway), it wasn't acceptable to return goods taken from one convenience store to another albeit in the same chain.

After three failed attempts, her faith seemed to be wavering.

When a cop confiscated her goods and threatened to arrest her for being a public nuisance, she zapped him with her reptilian tongue. At which point, his colleague sent a "police officer down" message to the nearest headquarters, earning us in short order a flock of pursuers.

We did what we could, traveled on side roads, exchanged license plates twice with parked cars, but every time we thought we had gotten away, there was someone else, some unanticipated pursuer behind us.

Mary alternated between rueful complaint and angry self-justification. One moment, she was ready to give herself up and the next she would chide me by saying, "If you had given me a baby this never would have happened."

"I liked you better when you were heartless," I said.

She stopped the car at the side of the road and told me to get out. When I refused, reminding her that I had a broken leg she said, "I hate you," and got out herself and walked off in the opposite direction, which is to say the direction of the pursuing car, which I recognized as it got closer.

It was the scientists and they drove slowly alongside Mary, one of them talking to her through an open window, urging her or so it seemed to come inside.

I was watching through my rear view mirror, feeling anxious, but not sure on whose account. Mary stopped momentarily to say something to her interlocutor when a flashing light, blindingly bright, emerged from one of the windows of the car.

When after several minutes, the light dissipated, Mary was gone, which is to say not even a telltale ash remained in the wake of her disappearance.

I felt oddly rueful all things considered and rolled down the window of my car to shout something incoherent at the scientists who seemed to be celebrating their accomplishment.

"If it weren't for you," one of them called to me, "we never would have gotten to her."

I tried to slide over into the driver's seat, but for each inch gained, the broken leg threw off spasms of pain. It might have been easier to get out of the car and edge my way around, using the sides of the car for balance, as a way of getting behind the wheel.

When the head scientist asked me where I was heading, I felt I knew the answer, that it was there waiting for me to access it, but I couldn't quite find the words to represent the thought. The encounter with the tree had scrambled my brains.

They offered to take me back to the hospital in their car, but I said I would be all right if they got me a walking stick. As it turned out, they had a spare one in the trunk of their van which they seemed pleased to give me. Nevertheless, I promised to return it as soon as my leg healed sufficiently to get around without it. I didn't want to be in debt to these murderers.

It was hard to get rid of them and since I could no longer remember where I had been going, I agreed to accompany them to this private sex club one of them knew about. Killing the dangerous alien, they told me, would not seem like the accomplishment it was unless they celebrated it appropriately.

I left my car at the side of the road and joined them in their van and we all drank cheap champagne and toasted one another as we drove through the night to wherever it was we were going—I could no longer remember—figuring it would pass the time until the sense of purpose I had lost revealed itself once again.

53rd Night

You had to wear a mask to get into what the scientists referred to as the Nameless Club and if you didn't bring one with you, you were asked to leave, or you wore the one they assigned you.

The scientists, who knew the drill, came prepared. The head man wore a mask of Peter Sellers as Dr. Strangelove. Another wore a mask of John F. Kennedy. The final two had on lifelike masks of vaguely recognizable second-line film stars.

Before we each went our own way, we agreed to meet at the entrance in exactly three hours.

I was issued the mask of an orangutan and I had to leave my driver's license with the doorman as hostage to its return. It was an eerie place—it could have been the set for a vampire movie—and in short order I regretted my decision to come along.

For a while I wandered around looking for a place to sit, but there were no chairs in the main hall. So I ended up leaning against a wall, watching the passing scene through the slit holes of my mask.

The main room, which was of ballroom size, was mostly dark except for a couple of large spinning balls overhead, which created a retro psychedelic effect. Though dance music was being piped in from somewhere, there were no dancers visible. Occasionally a paunchy man would approach one of the long-legged women, mumble something, and the couple would vanish moments later behind one of the closed doors.

Every once in a while, a uniformed figure would wander through the room with glasses of champagne on a tray, and though I was eager for a drink, none ever reached my corner of the room. Either all the glasses were claimed before the tray reached me or the server was intentionally avoiding me.

So I was at once thirsty and uncomfortable, having difficulty breathing through the microscopic nose holes of my mask, when a woman, one of the few under six feet tall, this one wearing a Nicole Kidman mask sidled up to me.

"You're the only one with a primate mask," she said. "It can only mean that they want to single you out. I'd get out of here if I were you."

I looked around me. I was in fact the only one in the large room with a non-human mask. "Who's they?" I asked.

"Take my arm," she said. "It'll look suspicious otherwise."

I took her arm and went with her through one of the closed doors at the side and then I began to wonder about her reasons for concerning herself with me in the first place.

There was another couple in the room, the man in Bruce Willis mask sitting in an overstuffed chair, the woman in Margaret Thatcher mask kneeling in front of him. They took no notice of our arrival.

My date led me by the hand to a couch on the far side of the room and before I knew it, I was asleep with my head on her lap.

When I woke, or was awakened, a paunchy man with the demeanor of a carnival barker was looming over us.

"What are we going to do with you?" he said to the fake Nicole in the hushed voice of authority. "We need this man, you know that, for our ceremony which commences {looking at his watch} in four minutes time."

I could feel my companion shiver under the weight of my head.

"Sir, he's not fit," she said. "He's running a fever and he has an injured leg as you can see."

"Does he?" he said. He poked my leg with the point of his shoe. "This is extremely awkward, given that our guests are expecting an appropriate subject. If he can't stand on his own two feet, I suppose we'll have to come up with a substitute. We can't disappoint our guests."

"I can stand up," I said, lifting my head just enough to see who I was dealing with—a small paunchy man wearing the mask of a demonic clown. "Would you get me my cane, which is on the floor behind you, I think."

"Up you go, cowboy," he said to me. "Let's see you stand."

I tried. I made the requisite effort, but it didn't happen. I stood on one leg in precarious balance before folding up onto the paunchy man's foot. He pulled his left shoe out from under me, making an odd, barely human sound in the process.

Moments after the paunchy man and my former companion left the room, two uniformed attendants appeared and lifted me from my resting place on the plush rug and, one holding my head, the other my feet, carried me from the room.

As they took me down the long corridor to the entrance, I could hear the paunchy man in the clown mask in the background, his voice amplified. "We have quite a turnout tonight for our burnt offerings sacrifice and I want to congratulate you all for being here. We are indeed fortunate to have a volunteer, a distinguished volunteer I might add for our service tonight. I'd like a well-deserved hand for..."

I never got the name. By this time, I was out the door in the moonless night, moving with bumpy dispatch, sweating from the cold, expecting to be dropped at any moment or rolled into the brush or whatever the grunting attendants had chosen for my final disposition.

54th Night

I woke slumped behind the wheel of my rental car, which had an empty space where the CD player had once held sway. I didn't allow it to matter. In most other ways, I was feeling improved. Waking up in opposition to the expectations you brought with you on going to sleep can be its own pleasure.

Then it struck me that the woman at the Nameless Club, who had saved me from some unspeakable fate, had put herself in danger as a consequence.

So I went off, retraced steps I had taken in another's car, to find the estate in the woods the team of scientists had taken me to for celebratory recreation.

I had no way of knowing how much time had elapsed—my watch had stopped at midnight (or was it noon?)—but I was driven by a sense of urgency. I drove for several miles without spotting the off-road turn we had taken—there had been a yellow reflector as landmark—and so I assumed I had missed it and I went back the way I had come. And then back again the other way.

I tried two side roads that led nowhere or at least not where I needed to go.

I stopped at a gas station and, after filling up, I asked the clerk in the connecting convenience store if he knew of an estate in the vicinity hidden from the road by high walls.

"That's funny," the clerk said, rubbing his chin. "You be the second person this morning to come into the store with the same question."

"And how did you answer him?" I asked.

"I didn't get no chance to tell him anything," he said, "because it was a woman not a man." He smiled slyly. "Didn't answer her either. Some men came in after her and she went off with them before I could say what I would have said."

"What would you have said to her?"

"You're kidding me, right?" he said. "I would have said I'm not from around here. You should ask my boss, but he's not on the premises at the moment."

"When's your boss coming back?"

"I don't expect him back," he said, "because he's already back. He's already back but he's in the back."

"Well, I'd like to talk to your boss," I said. "Does he ever make a personal appearance?"

"Yeah, no," he said. "Last time I called him out he nearly fired me."

I was about to give up, about to turn and leave when it struck me to ask him to describe the woman who had preceded me in inquiring about the estate.

The woman he described, or half-described—he was interrupted by the appearance of a vaguely familiar paunchy man emerging from a door in the back—sounded, allowing for his difficulty in expressing himself, as if she could have been Molly.

As the paunchy man approached the counter, the ache in my leg, which I hadn't felt for awhile, returned.

I decided not to pursue my inquiry and moved toward the door.

"Hey," the clerk said, "this is the man you wanted to as a question."

I was already by the door, had my back to the counter, when his voice stopped me. I turned slowly to get another look at the paunchy man, my mind exploding with possible questions, none of which seemed reasonable to ask. "It doesn't really matter," I say.

"I'm at your service," the paunchy man said, amused at something.

"Speak up. You may not get another chance."

I wondered if his remark was intended as a threat, which would have meant he had recognized me from the club. "I'm looking for a woman," I said.

"We don't have any in the store at the moment," he said. "Leave me your number and if one comes in, I'll give you a shout."

"He's been asking how to get to the club," the clerk said.

The paunchy man reached under the counter and I kept my eye on him as I backed out the door, noting what looked like a metallic object in his hand as it reemerged, though it may only have been a trick of the light. I didn't stay around for confirmation.

I figured they wouldn't shoot me in front of the two other cars gassing up. That was when I noticed that someone was in the driver's seat of my rental car, the face obscured by the light glancing off the window. It was fortunate that I couldn't run because I was three steps away when whoever it was started up the engine and the car in a belch of thunder exploded in flame.

55th Night

I stumbled away from the explosion, taking refuge in the woods, my movements obscured by the smoke. It struck me that once I was safely out of view, presumably presumed dead, that a rare opportunity was mine for the taking. I could shed my old identity and start over without any of the negative baggage the old self dragged around.

At first, overwhelmed by choices, I couldn't decide who or what I wanted to be, but then I thought why not a free-floating presence, a different identity for every occasion.

It was possible of course, though perhaps less than likely, that the authorities might not assume that I was the charred remains in the exploded car. So I continued on my way, pushing myself to go faster until it felt as though I had reached my limit.

My leg had been hurting so I snapped a branch from a dying tree to use as a makeshift cane.

I must have traveled about two miles when I heard voices up ahead. From what I could make out, there were two men, perhaps boys, and a woman and they were arguing about whether to go on or turn back.

I overheard the following conversation before revealing myself.

"Look," one of the boys was saying, "I'm not ashamed of being scared. If there's something out there that doesn't want us to go any further, I'm more than willing to take the hint."

"Oh, please!" the woman said.

"She's right," the other boy said. "Just because we find a corpse in the woods, it doesn't mean our lives are also at risk. Of course it doesn't. Besides, bad omens, dire warnings, scary moments are to be expected in an undertaking like ours."

"Keep your hands where I can see them," a voice behind me said. Someone had sneaked up on me from my blind side and was pressing a hard object that didn't feel like a gun into my back.

"Take it easy," I said. "I'm no danger to you."

"So you say," said the figure behind me. "Did Miriam, the dark-haired Miriam, send you? Don't turn around if you know what's good for you."

After he poked me again I gave his wrist a side of the hand chop, knocking whatever he was poking in my back (a green banana as it turned out) to the ground. His cry of pain brought the others in short order. They were older than I had imagined, in their early twenties perhaps, though I've never been good at determining age.

Although they seemed wary of me, the apparent leader of the group, a tall bald guy named Woodrow Kelp (called Woody), invited me to their campfire site, even offered me a charred marsh-mallow as a gesture of hospitality.

They were students working on a group project, the one called Larry told me, but that was the extent of my information.

"And who might you be?" I was asked.

I told them my name was Bud and that I was in the woods foraging for unusual mushrooms.

"What do you do when you find such mushrooms?" the woman, who was referred to by the others as Ms. M, asked in her sassy way.

"You don't seem to have any specimens with you at the moment."

"Oh I don't pick them," I said. "I see no reason to disturb the earth. I just make note of where they've been discovered and how they might be described."

I actually knew very little, virtually nothing about mushrooms, but this was the story that came to mind when Ms. M asked her question. What I was doing, as I saw it, was trying on a new identity.

They seemed to accept my story and I hung out with them for a while glad to have some company, and gradually, by fits and starts, twitches and throat clearings, they revealed the nature of their project.

They were students at a counter-cultural college for gifted misfits in New Hampshire that specialized in the study of unseen realities, or some such thing. This group of four were working together on a term paper for a class called The Dark Side of Human Behavior by investigating certain nasty inexplicable phenomena in the woods we had visited.

So far, all they had accomplished was the amassing of clues and omens, the latest and most disturbing of which was the corpse I had overheard them discussing.

I admired their courage, but I couldn't help but wonder if there wasn't something foolhardy, even self-destructive in continuing their pursuit. I withheld whatever discouraging remarks came to mind, not wanting to undermine their grim enthusiasm.

Finally, I asked Woody, the self-styled leader of the team, what they hoped to find at the end of their quest.

He took a deep breath before answering. "I don't exactly know," he said carefully enunciating each word, "because as yet it has no name."

He made a point of walking away from me before I could probe further. "And when you find the thing that has no name, what then?" I called after him.

Ms. M stole up to me and answered my question in a hushed voice.

"Like you with your mushrooms," she said, "we will not disturb the thing in any way. We are an investigating team. It is our job to locate and describe previously unknowable phenomena, not meddle with its destiny."

"What if the thing, as you call it, doesn't make the same distinctions?" I asked.

At first she brushed my question off with the back of her hand as being unworthy, but then she said, blushing in the faded light, "We are not without the ability to defend ourselves."

I was curious as to what she meant, but not curious enough to go much further with this quixotic group and I announced, thanking them for their company, that the time had come to go my own way.

"I'm sorry," Woody said as I started to walk away. "I'm afraid we can't let you go."

"What do you mean you can't?" I asked, though I didn't feel I needed permission to walk away.

"For one, you know too much," he said.

"Hey, I know nothing," I said. "I've been winging my way through life." But it wasn't knowledge of the world, or knowledge in general he was referring to. He meant—why hadn't I seen this right away?—that I knew too much about their project.

While I was overstating my support of their venture, someone sneaked up behind me and conked me with what may have been a club or an old hiking boot. When I came to, I found myself trussed from neck to toe by silken threads as though I were in a cocoon being carried along on a palette like a wounded soldier. So whether I liked it or not, I became a passive companion on their absurdly dangerous (perhaps dangerously absurd) adventure.

56th Night

I anticipated the two guys lugging me around on a stretcher would get tired of their assignment and it happened even more quickly than I expected.

The one they called Pill had been complaining all along, mostly under his breath about my weighing more than I should and how it was oppressing his back.

"What do you want to do with him then?" Larry said. "You got a better idea?"

"Sometimes—look, don't say anything to the others—I wish we weren't hamstrung by being non-violent," Pill muttered. "Anyhow, I got to answer nature's call, if you know what I mean."

So they put me down, virtually dropped me, and Pill went off in the woods somewhere to take a leak.

"The nerd drinks too much water," Larry said to me.

"How did you get this cocoon around me?" I asked him.

"Hey, that's one of Ms. M's little tricks," he said. "She's got a little spider in her, that girl. No more questions, okay?"

When Pill didn't return after what seemed like ten minutes, Larry called out to the others for help. There was no immediate response and it was beginning to get dark. "What do I do now?" he asked no one in particular, though I was his only audience. He raised his voice, took turns broadcasting Woody's name and Ms. M's name into the vast unknown, his voice echoing back at us the only response. Nerves got the better of him. He began to do a kind of twitchy dance to pass whatever time needed passing. "What do I do now?" he asked again.

In answer to his question, I suggested he untie me so there would at least be two of us against whatever.

He couldn't do that, he said, repeated it several times for emphasis before taking out a pocket knife and chopping at the spidery threads that held me.

Progress was slow—the strands difficult to cut—and I had only one arm free when Woody and Ms. M reappeared.

Woody took charge, suggested that instead of splitting up they all go together to look for Pill. Perhaps, said Ms. M, Pill, who had no sense of direction, had gotten himself lost by going the wrong way.

"What about this one?" Larry asked, meaning me.

I wasn't sure what I was hoping for or even what my best hopes might be in the present situation.

"It'll take too long to unravel him," Woody said, "so I think it best to just leave him here until we get back."

"Sorry," he said to me.

When they were gone, I picked up Larry's knife from the ground where he had dropped it and I used my free arm to saw away at the strands swaddling my legs. It was laborious work and I assumed they would be back before I made sufficient progress.

Hours seemed to pass without their return and I kept at it, though my arm began to ache, looking over my shoulder all the while, a kind of free floating urgency driving me.

Eventually, I was able to stand on one foot. Just as I was beginning to master the problem of remaining upright, I heard something moving in the brush, edging its way toward me.

I resisted panic, held my knife at the ready in case whoever it was intended me harm. And perhaps it was the group of young adventurers returning or at least the ones who had survived temporary disappearance.

To my surprise, a small, familiar, elderly woman appeared, brushing what seemed like spider webs from her clothing. I couldn't place her exactly, though I was sure we had met before. She resembled Molly more than a little, Molly twenty or so years down the road, a considerably older and cronelike version of my lost muse.

She greeted me with a cackle and an odd, almost benign smile. "You look familiar," I said. "Do I know you?"

"Do you think I'm attractive?" she asked.

I could see this was a delicate question and so I worked an answer over in my head, modifying it again and again so as not to seem either dishonest or hurtful. "You have a beguiling manner," I said at long last.

"I do what I can with what little I have," she said, the benign smile slipping from one side of the mouth to the other. "Would you like to dance with me?"

"I would," I said perhaps too quickly, "but I have a broken leg."

She considered my answer, seemed to chew on it while clearing her throat. "Is that a yes or a no?" she said, holding out her bony arms in my direction. For a fraction of a second, I thought of not taking her hands, though no other alternative offered itself and I could almost hear the sound of dance music coming from some incomprehensible distance away. And the next thing I knew we were whirling about to the distant strains, my bad leg keeping pace.

I put it down to illusion but she seemed to be getting younger as we danced in circles barely touching the earth as if the laws of gravity had taken the evening off. For a moment, I thought she had morphed into Ms. M.

I wondered as we flew in circles if she were responsible for the disappearance of the others. I also wondered if the same fate, whatever it was, was also what awaited me.

I asked her her name.

And then, momentarily, our dance took a horizontal turn and we were on the ground, my hard-on preceding a terrible awareness of desire. I held on to her pillowy ass with both hands as I entered her. "Come to me, masked man," she whispered.

And so we danced on the ground with my fickle prick between her legs which were wrapped around me like a ribbon. As soon as I came, the dance was over, the music silenced, and she, the unnamed, disappeared the way she came.

57th Night

My hair had turned white after the encounter with the crone who had emerged from the deep woods like an apparition. Insofar as I could tell, I was still alive, though conspicuously diminished.

By using the North Star as a reference point (and perhaps it was another star altogether), I gradually found my way back to the highway. My plan, which was the faded echo of what had got me here in the first place, was to hitch a ride into Maine. That was before I discovered that I was already in Maine having crossed the border in the course of my travels off the beaten track.

I needed to get myself together and with, rest in mind, I stopped off at the first motel that came my way, the Down Home Inn, which was owned and managed by a undernourished ornithologist. When he informed me that Cabin 13 was all he had available—the other quarters were in the process of being updated for a Virtual Reality convention—I knew I was in for a bad time.

I fell into a dreamless sleep on top of my covers (still in my clothes) and lost the world for several hours before being recalled by a series of heavy knocks on the door.

"Open the fucker up," a voice said, "or I'll break the fucker down."

"What do you want?" I found myself calling out, struck almost instantaneously that silence, a total refusal to acknowledge the intrusion, was a better way to go.

"You're in my room," the drunken voice called back. "Get your ass out of my room." He banged on the door with a heavy fist.

I looked around for my watch and couldn't find it in the dark, as if knowing the time would be a way of getting my bearings. It was at this point I opted for silence, assuming I was dealing with someone either drunk or mad.

"I'll break you in half, dickface," he shouted again after a momentary interlude in which I thought he had given up and gone away.

I called the office from my phone on the bed table and got a recording that advised me to keep trying.

My only hope was to outwait him and trust that whatever the door was constructed of would withstand his siege.

There were extended periods without the thumping but it always managed to return just when I thought he had given up and gone away.

Hoping the door was sufficiently well-constructed to withstand his assault, I returned to the bed.

No matter, I couldn't get back to sleep while the attempt to break down my door persisted.

Finally, I heard footsteps moving into the distance and I took a deep breath and closed my eyes.

I must have dozed because there was daylight coming through the curtain when I opened my eyes again.

I showered quickly, not wanting to leave myself in a vulnerable state, and dressed with similar dispatch into the alternate set of clothes I had on hand.

I was ready to see what faced me on the other side of the door when the phone rang.

Though I had no good reason to answer, the siren call got the better of me. "Who is it?" I said, avoiding the amenities.

"If I were you," a woman's voice said, "I'd get out of there in a magic minute."

Who am I running from this time I wanted to ask but there didn't seem any point so I hung up the phone and left the sanctuary of my room.

I stopped briefly to read the message scrawled in blood on the outside of the door. "GIVE IT UP," it said.

I hadn't taken two steps from the motel when a burly man well over six feet tall approached. I had noticed him asleep at the wheel of a truck parked near the office.

"I was the guy at your door last night," he said. "I don't remember what I said, but I hope you didn't take it to heart. I'm a notoriously unpleasant drunk." He held out his hand. "No hard feelings, okay?"

I shrugged. "You had me worried," I said.

"Look, ol' buddy, I'd like to make amends," he said. "It would make me feel a whole lot better if you accepted a lift in my truck to where you're going."

I said I wasn't sure where that might be since I didn't know which of the several resort islands in Maine the kidnappers had taken Molly.

"Don't worry, we'll find her," he said, "or my name isn't King Buck, which in fact it used not to be. You have to let me make it up to you. Please." He got down on one knee as if he was proposing.

Sober, he seemed harmless enough, and so, not without some residual reluctance, I accepted his offer.

"What kind of cargo do you carry?" I asked him.

"The female of the species," he said with a wry smile.

We hadn't gone very far when we hit a bump in the road and I noticed, in what must been a subliminal flash, inadvertently turning my head, a braceleted human arm spilling out from the tarp in the back that secured his otherwise hidden cargo.

58th Night

The trucker, who insisted I call him Buck, kept up a kind of jokey patter as we drove toward Vinalhaven, the first island on our itinerary, his third beer clutched in the hand that was unattached to the wheel. When we started out, Buck had warned me that it was dangerous to let him drink beyond his limit.

I thought this might be the time to say something.

"You probably have had enough, don't you think?" I said, putting my caution as delicately as I could.

"Where did you get the idea that a few beers was going to make some kind of fucking monster out of me?" he said in a voice I hadn't heard before except perhaps outside my door.

"It's what you told me," I said.

"I told you that?" he asked the now-empty bottle in his hand. "I guess I must be some kind of liar, huh?"

"I think I see her," I said, pointing to a twentyish blond just ahead, carrying a package under her arm. "You can drop me here if that's convenient."

The truck drove up to the woman so that Buck could get a better look at her. "Not too bad," he said, "but I think we can do better."

"I can get out anywhere here," I said, ignoring his odd remark.

A man came from the other direction and took the package from the woman and they went off together, arms around each other.

"What do you want to do about that?" he said as he trolled after the couple in his truck. "If she were my wife..." He left the thought unfinished.

"The sun must have been in my eyes," I said. "I can see now that she's not Molly."

"It's good you said something," he said, chugging his fourth beer, "because, hey, I was going to run that pretty boy down for you. Just kidding. Just as well. There's a causeway up ahead to the island. Don't worry. I'm not going to drop you before we get what we came for. Zum zum."

By this point, I was more than eager to get away from him but I could see that asking to be dropped off was a sure way not to get me what I wanted.

The island was larger than I imagined it would be. I did know from remarks Molly had made that the kidnappers were in possession of a lodge near the central marina.

There were two attractive women in a Cadillac convertible that pulled alongside us and Buck, keeping pace, danced his tongue at them in obscene gesture.

"Asshole," the one in the passenger seat called to him.

We followed them in the truck, kept them in sight for much of the time by going twenty miles or so an hour over the posted speed limit. They lost us briefly, but then we found their car in the parking lot of a seafood restaurant called Paradise One.

Buck parked the truck at the side of the road about 100 feet past the restaurant. He laid out a plan, which didn't make a lot of sense that had me going into the restaurant and convincing the women to join us in the truck.

I opened my door and I was getting ready to swing my legs over the side when he grabbed my arm. "You're coming back, with the babes or without, right?"

"Uh huh," I said.

"I'm not going to have to go in after you, am I?" he said, digging his fingers into my arm.

"Look, Buck," I said, pulling my arm free, "I'm not afraid of you."

He glared sternly at me, then in seeming slow motion, tears began to fall, big sloppy tears sluicing down his meaty face. I was appalled.

Before more tears spilled, I was out of the cab and working my way toward the Paradise restaurant and eventually inside. It was an overlit, undersubscribed place specializing, from what I could tell based on the plates that passed my way, in extravagant portions.

A cursory glance of the room did not readily reveal the two women I had been assigned to approach. What it did reveal was that Molly (or a woman who could have been her sister) was in a booth at the back with two men of disparate ages I had never seen before. She was sucking at the claw of a lobster.

She hadn't seen me, or hadn't let on that she had, and I took a booth which allowed, from a discreet distance, a privileged view of Molly's area of the room.

So as not to stick out, I ordered a fish burger—the waitress said it was the Specialty of the Maison—with home made generic cole slaw and sweet potato fries.

The longer I looked at Molly's back, the less sure I was that it was actually her. This lingering doubt proved an appetite depressant, so I decided to visit the Men's Room by way of Molly's table. In a neighboring booth were the two sexy women we had followed to the restaurant and they smiled in my direction as I passed.

I had almost reached Molly's booth when Buck appeared, sporting a sawed-off shotgun he had extracted before our eyes from under his red flannel shirt. "This is a stick-up," he announced. "You put your hands on the table where I can see them and no one will get hurt." He was so drunk he teetered from side to side, his open fly a cavern of false hope, as he slurred his announcement.

The small crowd ignored the outburst, went on eating as if nothing untoward had taken place, as if no plug-ugly six-foot-six intruder waving a shotgun had abruptly forced his way into their lives.

59th Night

When Buck started spraying the room with buckshot, those of us who weren't dead or immobilized got down under the tables to protect ourselves.

As soon as his ammunition ran out, Buck was taken into custody by a team of local police. Only to be released a few hours later when word came down that he was an undercover government agent on a mission so secret that only those in the highest of high places knew what he was about.

In the meantime, I got to be comforted by the two attractive women from the Cadillac convertible in the circumscribed space under their table.

When the shooting stopped and Buck was subdued, when the dust cleared and the wounded were carted away,. Molly and her two male companions were nowhere to be found.

My new friends and I exchanged stories and, finding one another sympathetic, we decided to make common cause. Toni and Win (Antonia and Winifred) had gone off on a vacation from stultifying domesticity—this was four years ago to the week—and for a conspiracy of circumstances had reached a point of no return. After running out of money, they kept themselves going by robbing convenience stores, limiting their thefts to basic necessities.

It was this moral component in their circumstantial life of crime that won me over to their predicament.

My story was as it had been: I was on a self-determined mission to rescue a former wife from her seemingly companionable kidnappers.

My part in the exchange of services was to drive the getaway car for an off-hours heist at an island supermarket.

It was an anxious wait on my part, sitting in the oversized convertible trying not to look conspicuous, but Toni and Win emerged fifteen minutes later empty handed. The supermarket had nothing they were willing to steal. "There's no point liberating over-the-hill bananas," Win complained.

We spent the night together in a motel room I had taken as a single, the women slipping in later under cover of dark.

So we shared the undersized double bed the room provided, taking turns being the one hugged in the middle. We gave the impression of liking each other to unwholesome excess.

The next day, we drove around the island looking for signs of Molly, checking out even the most unprepossessing roads. As a precaution, Win stayed in the motel in the morning while Toni made herself scarce in the afternoon. The wanted posters that had been circulating had pictures of them together as if inseparably joined at the hip and we thought this was the best way not to attract notice.

To wean Toni and Win away from their life of crime I paid for their meals with what I told them was a stolen credit card. They were resolutely opposed to accepting charity from anyone, particularly from a man. Their entire lives, Toni had confided, had been awash in emotional debt.

On the second afternoon of crisscrossing the island, I noticed, or thought I did, Molly (or a woman who resembled Molly), walking a small white dog of familiar if indeterminate breed.

Why didn't I say something to Toni? Why didn't I ask her to drop me off or to turn down the road and follow the woman with the pet dog? I have no answer to those questions, but the fact is I said nothing. It's possible that I wanted to stay with Toni and Win one more night, which was the way it played out.

Toni and Win were planning to leave the island late the next day—they were careful about not staying in the same place too long—after giving the search for Molly one further extended try.

I was with Win this time when I saw Molly park her bicycle at the central marina and board a sailboat called Lothario. There were two others also on board, but I couldn't tell if they were the same two I had seen with Molly at the Paradise One Restaurant.

My plan was to come back after Toni and Win had gone off and wait for Molly where the Lothario had been anchored.

When we returned to the motel, we said our goodbyes, one hug leading to another, two hugs leading to one last roll in the bed. It was that hard to separate. And I knew I couldn't go with them, much as I might have wanted to.

At first I thought the sounds were coming from us, only louder this time and longer lasting, the amplified sighs of exhausted pleasure, but to think so had been a useful self-deception.

I was in the bathroom when the gunfire started—Win had just stepped outside to load the car. I could almost swear I heard Buck's voice saying, "On the count of three, let the shit rain." The shelling of the motel went on for at least five minutes—I later learned there were fifteen expert marksman shooting at us—which was when I lost consciousness, which was when the dream of death flashed before me only to be obliterated by the black hole that followed.

After the ambush at the hotel, nothing would be the same again, but wasn't it always that way.

PART TWO

(Confessions)

68th Night

The doctors lie when they say I have no memory. Look, I remember everything. To tell them they have it wrong is only going to make them angry so I keep this wisdom to myself. It could be that I have already told the doctors they lie and it slipped my mind. It is also possible that the doctors say I have no memory (while knowing it isn't true) to protect me from the team of interrogators who refuse to believe my answers to their questions.

Something happened to me a while back from which I haven't fully recovered. I am strapped to a cot in what appears to be a hospital ward, though that was true yesterday. It may be true again tomorrow. Reality changes in this place from day to day, from hour to hour.

"What is this place?" I sometimes want to know.

"We're the ones that ask the questions, dummy," the interrogators say.

I like that they call me dummy. It is something to hang on to, a familiar name. Otherwise, I am no one.

The interrogators—there are three who interchange—like to get the answer they are looking for, the one they have in mind before they ask the question. I do my best to please, but my best tends to fall short.

An example: they've asked on several different occasions where I met Antonia and Winifred for the first time and when this meeting took place. Each time, they've asked, I've come up with a different answer, which is always, it seems, the wrong answer.

It stands to reason if I keep on inventing new answers, eventually I'll hit on the right one.

If I get it right, they tell me, if I tell the truth (meaning their truth), the quality of my life while strapped to this cot would improve immeasurably.

On certain days, I never know in advance which ones, visitors are allowed.

Today, as a matter of fact (perhaps it is no longer today), my parents, recently dead, come to see me.

"The authorities informed us of your accident," my mother says. "Your father and I were most unhappy to hear of it."

"What did they say?" I ask, wanting to get the whole picture or at least complete the patchy jig saw puzzle I carry around in my head..

"Well," my mother says.

"We can't say anything," my father says. "We've been sworn to secrecy."

My mother winks as if to say wait until old stick-in-the-mud is out of the room.

Moments later, as if on cue, my father announces he's going to the men's room, having rushed from home without taking time to do his business. My parents embrace and tears fall on both sides before my father actually departs.

"So?" I say to my mother when we're alone.

"What so?" she asks, so I spell it out for her. I need to know what the authorities said about me.

"Please," she says. "Are you asking me to betray your father? Is that what you're asking your mother to do. In a marriage, if one person has a deep dark secret, so has the other. That's the nature of a marriage."

"Not really," I say.

"I will never betray your father without his permission," she says. "What did I always tell you when you were a child?" she says.

"There was more than one thing," I say, curious as to what she has in mind.

"I distinctly remember telling you on several occasions: you can never go wrong, son, by telling the truth people want to hear."

I can't remember her ever saying that to me, but maybe she has.

"What if you don't know what the truth is?" I ask her.

"That's the kind of question that's gotten you in trouble before," she says, "isn't it? Everyone has a right to make a mistake once if they admit it afterwards."

At this point my father returns, drying his hands on the side of his pants. "I can see something's going on here," he says. "What has mother said to you behind my back?"

"Nothing bad," I say. "Nothing about you."

"What did you tell him?" he asks her.

"The two you," she says, "you're so much alike which is why you're so suspicious of each other."

"What did you tell him?" he says as if it were the recording of the first question.

"I told him," she says, winking at me, "that your father and I believe that if you tell them the truth, they'll let you come home to us."

"Nah," my father says. "Don't listen to your mother. The truth won't do you any good. You tell them what they want to hear, you hear me. Now we have to go, I'm sorry to say. You're not our only child."

Funny. I thought I was.

"If dad says so, it must be so," she says without perceptible irony.

In a flash, they're out the door, my mother blowing a kiss, my father saluting.

Dinner doesn't arrive at the usual time, but of course the wall clock has stopped and so my only gauge of time is whether I'm hungry or not. Not is the preferred alternative. They haven't fed me in a dog's age.

When there is food, I usually spend the first hour or so trying to identify its source.

Soon the interrogators will return, sometimes in a group of three (in reverse size place), more often one at a time and I will be urged to confess yet again.

I work on a confession that could well be appropriate to whatever they might ask.

67th Night

"Fuck you," I answer. It is the voice of outrage speaking.

"Fuck you is not going to get it done," the number two interrogator (he's the Klaus Kinski type with the ripe German accent) says. "You want to get your hands untied, you got to do better than that. I wouldn't be at all surprised if your arms were coming out of their sockets."

"Please untie me," I say. "I'll give you what you want."

"You got to give us something first," says the head man.

"Why don't you untie him," says number three, who is a woman and less abrupt in her manner than the others. "If you don't get what you want, you can always tie him up again. I think he 's ready to cooperate." She puts her hand on my crotch.

"Yesterday, you told us you knew those girls in high school," number one says. "The thing is, we know Winifred and Antonia didn't go to the same high school. So what's the real story?"

"Fuck you is the real story," I say.

"You're a terrorist, aren't you?" two says.

I'm wondering which answer will get them to untie me. "No," I say, which induces no response. "Actually, yes."

"Were the girls working with you?" the woman asks.

"I don't know," I say. "Yes."

"Cut him down," one says. They look around for a knife, find a pair of scissors in one of the drawers and, after a few agonizing minutes, cut the ropes, permitting me to lower my arms.

I am prepared to tell them anything not to have my arms strung to the pipe thing again.

"Did they take orders from you or you from them?" one asks, placing a recorder on the edge of the bed.

"Sometimes one way, sometimes the other," I say. "They were

driving alone in their open car and when they noticed me on the side of the road with my thumb in the air, they slowed down."

"And when was that?" two asks, interrupting my train of thought.

"Five years ago," I say.

"You've known them for five years?" the woman asks, seemingly surprised by my answer.

"Perhaps it was three years ago," I say.

They look at their notes, huddle in the far corner of the room. Buzz buzz buzz buzz. "In our first interview," says the woman, "you said you only knew them for a short while. Were you lying then or are you lying now?"

"In my profession," I say, "which I have only the vaguest recollection of having practiced, I feel obliged to tell whatever seems the best story at the time."

The interrogators leave the room, the woman returning moments later. "When you say 'in my profession,'" she asks, "what profession exactly are you referring to?"

The answer comes to mind, then slips away. "Don't you know?" I say. "Who do you think I am?"

"It's an old trick," she said, "to try to turn the tables on the questioner. Would it be accurate to say that the profession you're referring to is the commission of seemingly random acts of violence? Please answer if you don't wish to be tied again with your arms in the air. I think you know that I'm the only friend you have in here."

"I appreciate your kindness," I say, only half aware that I am dissembling. "The profession I was referring to is that of storyteller."

"You are saying that you're a professional liar, is that it?" she says, turning away. "And I was beginning to like you, sweetheart." She takes a tiny cell phone from her pocket to answer a call or perhaps to make one.

The word "storyteller" makes itself known from time to time.

"Look, I am not a professional liar," I say when I have her attention again, "though I admit there is a connection between liar and teller of stories."

I confess that I have violent mood swings and a bad temper and that a former therapist said—I think he meant it in a positive way—that I tend to be self-involved.

"That isn't anything I want to know," she says. "Unless…"

"Unless?"

"Unless it was your uncontrollable temper that got you into the situation we're talking about," she says.

"I made every effort to avoid fights because of my temper," I say. "I knew that once I got started I wouldn't be able to stop myself. So I avoided all provocations except for this one time." I have no idea what I am going to say so I pretend I am censoring myself from telling the story while at the same time trying to come up with something vaguely credible.

"Were you with Toni and Win when this happened, storyteller?" the woman asks.

"I must have been," I say. "I mean, your asking me about them must have stirred up this memory. That makes sense, doesn't it?"

She turns on the tape recorder, which she holds out in my direction and clicks it on. "I'm listening," she says, but that isn't what she means.

"One of them was dancing with this drunk aggressive guy who was leaning into her. It might have been that I was the guy. I don't think so. I think it was someone else and that I was sitting across from them. I had the sense that Win was appealing to me to help."

"Where was Toni?"

"I think she was in the bathroom at this time. The drunk—he was a big guy, burly—forced Win to go outside with him. I seemed to be the only one aware of what was going on, which urged a certain responsibility on me, wouldn't you say. Win had this imploring look on her face."

"Did she?" the woman says. "Would you repeat that? You had your head turned. …Questioner is asking prisoner to repeat his remarks."

"So I went outside to see what was going on."

"Was this man who was in your words forcing Win to leave the establishment in his custody a law enforcement officer"

"If he was, and I can't be sure one way or another, he wasn't wearing a uniform."

"Describe what the man was wearing."

I'm not very observant so even if my memory was working on all gears, I wouldn't be able to answer her question. "He had on a plaid shirt," I say, "and shit-kicking boots."

"And as you say, you followed them outside. Is that right? To what purpose?"

"To protect her if there was no other way."

"And why would you think she needed protection? The man, who you say was forcing her, might have been taking her outside in his capacity as a law enforcer. Isn't that a possibility?"

"You're right, of course," I say. "I'm just describing what I saw and what I did."

"Go on."

"I didn't see them at first but then I heard what sounded like a call for help and I went in the direction it was coming from. I was holding a wrench in my hand, though I'm not sure how I acquired it."

"Go on."

"The woman, Win, was being shoved into the back of an SUV parked at the side of the road. I could see bruises on her face where she had been punched. When her assailant saw me coming towards them, he pointed a gun at me and said to mind my own business if I knew what was good for me. I don't know why but I kept moving toward him and then Win bit his hand and the gun came loose. Crying out, her assailant hit her with his fist knocking her head into the back of the car. The other woman, Toni, who I hadn't seen before, picked the gun up off the ground."

"Where did Toni come from? You said she was in the restroom."

"Well, maybe it was Win who had picked up the gun and Toni was somewhere behind me coming on to the scene."

"He had just knocked Win unconscious, how could she have

picked up the gun?"

"I take your point. It wasn't likely that Toni would have gotten to the gun before me. So I must have been the one to pick up the fallen gun. I had never fired a hand gun before and my intent was to rescue Molly, although it was Win this time, wasn't it, by keeping the gun away from her assailant. Win wasn't moving so I gave the gun to Toni, who had just come up behind me and told her to cover me while I carried Win to safety. Before I could react, Buck, I think that was his name, had Win in a stranglehold and was using her as a shield. And then I noticed that two of his redneck friends had come out of the bar and were calling to him and we had lost whatever limited advantage we had."

"I'm losing you," the interrogator says.

"When Toni shot Buck in the leg, Win was able to free herself and we got into a pink Cadillac convertible which had been left unattended about a hundred feet away."

"So you admit to having stolen the car."

"Yes, but we would have returned it if given the chance. The three of them chased us in Buck's Blazer and we exchanged gunfire and I got lucky and must have blown out a tire because their van went off the road and crashed into a tree."

"And after that you stopped to see if anyone had survived the crash."

"No. Not that I remember. I think we just continued on."

"Didn't you want to know what happened to your pursuers?"

An image flashes before my eyes of a large man slumped over a steering wheel, his face crusted in blood. The interrogator removes her blouse and sits down on the side of the bed. She removes her bra and invites me to put my head between her breasts. I am not usually so reticent. An unseen hand lingers on my crotch as if it were the only possible resting place.

"I wanted them dead," I say. "I killed them all. I fucked both girls that night."

"You lovely man," she says.

60th Night

The following is the transcript of my first confession. They write down everything you say here. No falsehood, no specious sigh, is left unrecorded.

I was hired and subsequently trained by an ultra-secret sub-government organization as an assassin. I was at loose ends at the time and looking to do something adventurous. For some reason, perhaps shyness, I never bothered to verify the credentials of the shadowy men that hired me.

Initial contact was established through an unstamped letter dropped through my mail slot, offering me the opportunity for well-paid, fulfilling work with the added bonus of exotic travel while serving the unannounced interests of my country.

Nothing in the recruiting flyer suggested that killing might be part of the job description. The offer came with a questionnaire, which would indicate or not whether I had the right stuff for the job. I filled out the questionnaire in my usual fanciful way and expected of course never to hear from whoever it was again. Three weeks later I got a check in the mail for fifty dollars, which if signed and deposited would represent acceptance of their offer including an all-expenses-paid invitation to their training facilities in New Mexico.

I agonized over the decision, but when a week later a check for two-hundred dollars arrived in the mail, I provisionally accepted their offer.

The training was very much like the preparations for the football season at my high school. A lot of it had to do with the testing and sharpening of reflexes. A notable exception was the weaponry work in our regimen. I suppose I should have known that if they put guns in your hands for practice, eventually they'll ask you to use them for real. The thing is, they kept us so busy we didn't have time to reflect on the implications of what we were doing.

Anyway, my weaponry instructor, a woman virtually my own age, was very encouraging, complimented virtually everything I did in the shooting-at-human-targets class, said I had a natural gift for this kind of work.

My first assignment was to serve as my final exam for the course so they sent a shadowy figure with me to grade my performance.

I assumed that this would not be a actual assassination, just a realistic approximation, that we were just going through the motions to test how well I had assimilated the training. Consequently, it was a shock to discover, watching the news on TV that night, that the public figure I had lined up in the sights of a high-powered rifle had been shot between the eyes from some unseen distance.

The discovery threw me into a funk and my immediate supervisor sent me home for rest and recovery. Eventually, obsessive regret turned into amnesia and I felt absolved for whatever it was I had done. So I was feeling okay about myself when my second assignment arrived through the mail slot in my door in an unstamped envelope.

The assigned target was a public figure I had always instinctively disliked so I thought to myself, I'll do this one for the payday and then quit, change my name (which they had already changed) and go somewhere unexpected, a place no one would think to look.

As much as I disliked the target, and possibly for that very reason, I couldn't kill the man when faced with the opportunity. It made no sense, but that's the way it was.

When I reported my failure to my superior, she said not to move from the booth I was phoning from, that they would send someone I knew to bring me in for debriefing. The someone they sent, a man I had trained with in New Mexico, took a shot at the phone booth from a roof across the street.

Fortunately, or unfortunately, there was someone else in the booth at the time. Instinct had led me to wait elsewhere.

When they discovered their mistake, they came after me again, and again, and in the process, mostly in self-defense, I ended up killing more people (sometimes bystanders got caught in the cross-fire) than if I had continued my aborted career as assassin.

So the killing didn't stop, as I had hoped, but became a way of life predicated on the instinct to survive, the body count far beyond anything I could have imagined.

When the secret government agency got tired of sending their own operatives after me, they framed me for capital crimes in places I sought sanctuary so that the local authorities would do the job for them. Even in places I had never been before, I was an established public enemy, thought to be armed and dangerous, my face on file on virtually every electronic screen.

During this period, I was in constant motion, eating and sleeping on the move, so tuned to impending danger that everyone on my radar screen seemed a potential assassin.

If there was no safe place to go, the only way to break the pattern was get myself killed. The idea came to me when I met this derelict, who looked enough like me to pass as my twin. This is not a story I am particularly proud of so I will not go into the unappetizing details.

Suffice to say, a week or so after I was reported dead, the agency that hired me and had been doing their damnedest to get me off their books, gave up their pursuit.

When I surfaced again with a new identity, new fingerprints, new face, I was a free man until unfortuitous circumstance dumped me in your lap, if indeed you are the same bloody-minded super-secret agency that I worked for in happier times.

73rd Night

They must have believed something I told them. Today Molly, who has been eluding me for the longest time, waltzes into my room. Her appearance, if anything, is an even greater surprise than the visit last week from my dead and cremated parents. Is it a good surprise? Any company in this place, even the company of someone who has lost all her illusions about you, is better than being alone.

"I was hoping to rescue you from your kidnappers," I say, "but as you can see I got kidnapped myself on the way. They keep pressing me to confess but then they don't believe what I tell them."

"Before we go any further," Molly says, "I need to get this said. Okay? This is not intended as a friendly visit."

"No?" I say, reaching out an imaginary hand to her (my hands are tied behind my back), which she slaps away, "Anyway, I'm pleased to see you."

"Every time I see you, I feel angry," she says. "It makes me angry to feel angry all the time. I know you understand what I'm saying, though I also know you'll do your best to pretend not to know what I mean... I'll tell you what I'm here for. I'd like to review our time together so I can internalize the total experience and so, you know, move on. You owe me this, okay?"

"You've already moved on," I say. "You've moved on and on and on."

She cries, a sudden unpredictable change in the weather, a local storm with larger implications. "I can't do this by myself," she says. "Will you help me or do I have to go back into therapy with the hormonal Dr. F?"

She puts on her recently removed denim jacket, which resembles— I have been noting this since her arrival—a former jacket of mine.

"You dumped me for greener pastures," I say.

"Not at all," she insists. "You may have been my greenest pasture. Anyway, the abominable Dr. F says the process will only work if we start from the beginning. So?"

There is no beginning, I want to say, or this is the beginning. Instead, I apologize for not having lived up to her expectations.

"I told Dr. F that it was a mistake to come here," she says. "Everything is amusing to you, even pain. You have no capacity for..." She leaves the sentence unfinished. "Did we like each other when we met. I can't remember. We must have, don't you think?"

"We met in a supermarket," I say. "You asked me why I had only one item in my cart. I didn't think it was any of your business but I was too polite to say so. The next thing I know we were in a motel room together."

She smiles wistfully through her tears. "We had a catch," she says, "do you remember, with a balled up pair of socks before we made out."

"It sounds familiar," I say, "but I remember it not as socks but as rolled up silk panties. Even in a ball, they were hard to hold on to. They had no weight."

"It was socks," she insists. "You were showing off and throwing the ball—the ball of socks—behind your back."

"It could have been socks," I allow.

"It was totally socks," she says. "And how did we get from throwing the socks back and forth into the bed?"

"One of my errant behind the back throws landed on the bed," I say. "Then we each made a mad dash to the bed, each of us hoping to retrieve the socks before the other."

"I have this flash image in my mind of you pushing me out of the way," she says. "You were always so competitive."

The way I remember it, Molly was the one pushing me out of the way.

"After the pushing, whoever was doing it, there was a readjustment of priorities.

We forgot about the socks and the socks forgot about us."

"That's your story," Molly says. "Even while we were making love, I was thinking that as soon as this is over, I'm going to get my hands on the socks before he does."

"For me," I say, "the love-making interlude in a socks-catching game has more enduring interest than the game itself. You know, I don't remember where we went from there."

"I went back to graduate school," Molly says, "and we wrote letters back and forth. That was a time when people still wrote letters. Between the letters, when the socks were still floating in the ether of memory, we each married different people."

I had forgotten all of this. It's hard for me to remember anything when my hands are tied behind my back. Still, it's a relief not to have my arms strung up over my head, which was the former regimen. "Am I right in thinking that the people we married were not the kind to throw smelly balled-up socks back and forth?" I say.

"You were the only one I ever had a socks catch with," she says. "I lost my socks-catching virginity with you. And then we met again wholly by chance. Is that the way you remember it? We had to have met somewhere or we never would have ended up married to each other. No?"

"It seems to me," I say, "that we never met again, though managed to get married anyway."

"That's why we didn't last," Molly says. "We didn't last because nothing is serious to you."

"Everything is too serious to take seriously," I say, feeling misunderstood.

"When we made connection again you were sitting next to me and you were jabbing me with your elbow. You were born with a sense of yourself as someone with a divine right to public armrests."

Molly sticks her tongue out at me in unspoken dispute. "After the movie," she says, "the four of us went to a restaurant together. When no one was looking, I stuck a card with my phone number on it in your jacket pocket."

"So we ended up in a motel room again," I say, "though this time it was a hotel, wasn't it? And there was another ball of socks catch."

"That's not the way it was," Molly says. "When I was getting back into my clothes, you threw your balled up socks at me. 'Think fast,' you said. There was no back-and-forth, nothing that might be construed as a socks-catching episode. When you hit me in the breast with your socks, it touched me. I knew in that moment that it would take me years to get free of you. ...Look, I forgot to mention it. They're recording this conversation. They wouldn't have let me in unless I agreed."

I make no complaint.

"Anyway," she adds, "they say it's for training purposes only."

"Doesn't matter," I say. "I've long since run out of shameful stories to tell them,"

"A few months after your socks touched my heart," she says, "we were living together. In memory, it seems like the next day, and also as if it never happened."

"I only threw socks at you for training purposes," I say.

"Right," Molly says. "Our life together was for training purposes. We lived together for two years, for more than two years, before we made it official. In all the time we were together, I can't remember you ever throwing socks at me again."

Could that be true? "Do you think our marriage an anti-climax, that all the good stuff happened before we were married?".

Molly sits down on the side of the bed next to me and pokes me with her finger. "I could do that all day and you couldn't hit me back."

"Forget it," I say.

"All through our marriage," she says, "I had this feeling that something was missing. This feeling, this absence, is something I've been carrying around with me forever. It was all anti-climax after our first time. Whimsical episodes become mawkish when willfully repeated."

I am suddenly distressed by the turn in the conversation. "Then why did you move in with me?" I ask. "Why did you live with me as long as you did?"

"If I knew the answer to that question," she says, "I wouldn't have bribed my way in here to see you."

"You stayed with me," I say, having what seems like a moment of clarity, which I immediately distrust, "to collect information. You were teaching yourself to know what to avoid the next time around."

"You goose," she says almost affectionately. "You never understand me because you're too busy reading other people as if they were less subtle versions of yourself. Given the same opportunities, I most likely would play out our time together all over again. Some things can't be usefully avoided. Isn't that so?"

"If I knew anything useful," I say, "I wouldn't be in this awful room with my hands tethered behind me... So why did you dump me after what was it, eight years together, nine, seven, eleven?"

"For the usual reason," Molly says, slightly abashed. "There was someone else."

Now we're getting somewhere, or nowhere. I hesitate before asking the inevitable next question. "And why was there someone else?"

"I'm figuring it out," Molly says, hunkering down on the narrow cot. "There was someone else because I needed to dump you."

"Isn't that a circular argument?" I can feel the heat of her body next to me, though we are not actually touching.

"What if it is," she says. "I'm feeling like I'm getting what I came for."

"And?" I ask, unable to remember the reasons offered for the visit.

"It no longer matters," she says. "Close your eyes, sweetheart, and let the past forget us."

I don't close my eyes and then I do—what else is there to do in this place—and then nagged by a discovery that refuses to stay in focus—I open my eyes one at a time, an extended interval between right and left, aware of her absence before registering that she is actually gone.

There is someone else in the room, the number three interrogator, watching me from a dark corner.

94th Night

It's been so long since my last visitor, I can no longer remember having ever been visited. The tray with my inedible food is slipped under the door whenever they remember I'm still here. Not even an interrogator has come by in a while to ask the idle probing question. I suspect the word on the street is that I've already sung all the songs I have in me to sing. What do they know? Really?

The texts of confessions I haven't yet made, haven't even thought of before this moment, keep running through my mind. I've been to the north pole of violation and back and the worst of it is, the most unforgivable, is that there's no one to tell about it. You reach a point in this place where you would gladly put up with some official nastiness just for the company.

"If you've lost your interest," I shout at the recording system in the wall, "send me home."

Toward evening, two attendants deliver another cot to what had been for some time now a private room.

When they first brought me here, there was a second bed in the room occupied by an almost skeletal figure. He never spoke, though tended to let out heart-rending moans during the night. A day or so after the moaning stopped—changes tend to happen in the dark here—I woke one morning to find bed and occupant disappeared. When I asked the interrogators about my roommate's absence, they insisted no one else was ever in the room with me.

The new guy is a lot younger, a teenager maybe, but it's hard to tell his age. He's painfully thin, virtually emaciated, has an IV in his arm. At first, jealous of my space, I don't acknowledge him. When the silence becomes intolerable I hear myself say, "How's it hanging, bro?" I mean what else is there to say to someone you don't know who's moved into your room uninvited.

"Do I know you?" he asks, his yards of unearned self-assurance intolerable.

The question attacks a nerve, makes me immediately suspicious though I couldn't say what of. "You don't know me," I say. "Do I look like someone you know?"

"Everyone looks like someone I know," he says.

"You know what I think, kid. I think they put you in here to spy on me."

He laughs, which breaks into a wracking cough. "If I have," he says, "no ass-wipe bothered to tell me about it. You know, Pops, you've always been fucking paranoid."

"What do you mean always, kid?" What does he mean always? I take another look at him (watch him out of the side of my eye) to see if I know him. He looks like any other emaciated nineteen-year-old. "Look, you can't say always to someone you've just met."

"Who says I can't?" he says. "Fuck anyone who says I can't."

After that we stop talking, each pretend we're alone in the room. Later in the day, though it could be the next day, the number three interrogator makes an unscheduled appearance. I salute her as she enters, but she ignores me and sashays over to the interloper's bed.

"I like the way you've done your hair," I call to her.

She gives me one of her characteristic inscrutable smiles. "Put a sock in it," she whispers, returning her attention to the boy. "Has everyone here treated you well?" she asks. "You'd tell me, wouldn't you if anyone here abused you."

He shields his mouth with his hand, presumably to keep me from hearing him. "The guy with the beard on the other side of the room," he says.

"It won't happen again," she says. "You have my promise, Tick. Tick—you like to be called Tick, isn't that right?—I have a few questions for you. Your answers are very important to us so be careful to tell us the whole truth as you know it."

"Tick's got nothing to hide," he says.

The interrogation goes on for a while and I do my best to tune it out—a pillow over my head doesn't quite do it—and it drives me bananas hearing her ask the kid the same questions more or less they asked me when I was their favored suspect.

At the close of the interrogation, she puts her hand between his legs and kisses him on the forehead, which is unacceptable in my view. This is only his first on site interrogation. It wasn't until my third that I got the forehead kiss and the hand on prick caress, which in my case turned out to be a false promise.

After she leaves, he has this shit-eating smile on his face, which further intensifies my displeasure with him. "Kid, she touched my prick too," I tell him. "It's no big deal. From what I can tell, she probably does the same thing with everyone she questions."

"Hey Pops," he says, "I know it's no fun to be left out. Look, I want to say I'm sorry, you know, your day is over. When it's over, it's over, Pops. Lights out."

I don't want to get into a pissing contest with the kid so I turn on my side away from him while a slew of witty retorts crowd the inside of my head. "And don't you ever call me Pops again," I say under my breath.

"Anything you say, Pops," he says, snorting air.

I wake up from a brief nap, sniffing smoke. "Who's smoking? There's no smoking allowed in this room."

The kid brushes the smoke away with one hand while holding what looks like a cigarette behind his back. "You've been dreaming, old man," he says. "Whatever smoke you think you see in this room is a natural part of the atmosphere."

I see what's going on. They've put the little bastard in here to aggravate me, to break me down and my only revenge is to not let that happen. I sit up and I wonder if my legs will hold me if I climb off the bed. At the same time, he is also working his way off his bed with the intent (the same as mine) of reaching the floor in an upright position.

It would be hard to prove without an exceptionally precise slow-motion replay, but I am the one who gets to his feet first. I am fractions of a second ahead of him. The business of balance is tricky. I sway from one side to the other, watch myself teeter in the echo of his totter. I am, I believe, ready to risk my first step.

I watch him stumble while awkwardly, at seeming great risk, retain his precarious balance.

We are now moving irrevocably toward the other, though in what seems like mock slow motion, huffing and raging, while making virtually no progress.

As we get closer, I work on the rudiments of a defensive strategy.

Perhaps if I punch him in the face before he can land the first blow, it will be sufficient to claim victory. It strikes me that it might be prohibitively difficult to maintain my balance while thrusting my clenched fist in his direction.

"Back off," I say to myself, to him, to myself, but he keeps approaching and so do I, so it is hard to tell who is closing the distance faster.

We are at the moment no more than two small hesitant steps apart.

As the space between us recedes, I trip and fall toward him with my arms out. "Watch it, Pops," he says.

"Watch it yourself."

We grab at each other as we meet, holding on to keep from falling, caught by the hidden camera in a parody of an embrace.

95ᵗʰ Night

They come during the night, two men in stocking feet, and lift me out of the bed, while I am still, for all they know, asleep and carry me between them down a narrow hallway that seems to go on forever. We are serenaded by night cries from unseen quarters as we shuffle along to a door that leads to a narrower hallway and thento another door. And through the second door into the moonless night.

I am dropped off onto the back seat of a black van which stays in place only long enough for the door that admitted me to be slammed shut.

I have been pretending to be asleep, though I'm not at all sure if it's the most useful way to go on this occasion. This is the first time I've been outside the prison/hospital complex since they brought me here blindfolded, however long ago it was.

A heated discussion goes on in the front seat between a man and a woman—the man in the driver's seat—in a language that is not one of mine.

It's all in the tone of voice. As I hear it, the man is arguing for a quick and painless slaughter while the woman supports a more subtle and dire retribution.

After a while—perhaps I've misunderstood all along—I am pulled out of the car from behind and dumped like a bag of trash in the wet spiky grass of an overgrown field.

"You are lucky soldier," the woman calls to me in heavily accented English moments before the unmarked van races off, spraying exhaust and dirt in its wake.

I collect myself as if I were several different random parts held together with tape.

The exhilaration of being my own man once again lasts a few

ragged moments. "I am free man," I say to myself in imitation of the woman's fake accent. No doubt, they've left me here to die.

I don't know how much time has passed when someone—perhaps the wind—asks, "Are you alive?"

When I open my eyes (how else can I know?) there is a small person—perhaps a child—standing over me, prodding me with a long stick.

"What about you?" I say. "Are you alive?"

He takes a step back, offering in the process a barely perceptible nod.

I hold on to the end of his stick. "You have any food, a cookie, chips, fruit, nuts, anything?"

He takes another step backwards, testing his options, looks as if he's about to run away. Then slowly, divesting himself of his stick, backing up as if I might not notice if he were quiet about it, he edges away.

I do what I can to keep up, move after him on all fours. He can lose me if he wants to, but he turns back from time to time to keep me in sight. Or so I interpret his turn of the head gesture until at some point he flat out vanishes.

"Hey," I hear myself say, but when the thin echo of sound is gone, it's hard to imagine it ever was.

I continue in my subhuman locomotion, hoping to pick up his trail when the indistinct path I seem to be following splits off into two opposing indistinct paths.

Too weak to make a meaningful choice, I lie down at the crossroads and listen to myself breathe as if it were the latest news.

It may be five minutes later, it may be the next day, but the child—the boy—is standing over me again. a larger person at his side. The larger person has something round in her hand which she extends in my direction.

I assume it is some kind of food and, in no condition to be picky, I reach out for it with open mouth, rotted teeth at the ready.

The larger person pulls back her hand with a startled cry and whatever she was holding drops to the ground, unclaimed on either side.

The boy retrieves what may be an apple and holds it close to my face (for inspection?), an inch or so from my mouth.

After sniffing my prize to determine that it is as sight advertises, there seems nothing else to do but take a bite out of the apple.

The boy claps his hands, jumps up and down, and I have to pull my head out of the way to avoid an approving pat.

"Can we?" the boy says. "Please."

"If it will make you happy," the woman says, not without some reluctance. "I'm going to need your help, Bobby. I can't take something like this on all by myself."

They help me to my feet, and I am upright for a few seconds before collapsing to the ground.

"Don't fall too far behind," the woman says to one or both of us as I follow them on all fours to a cabin in the deep woods where the boy and his mother apparently live.

Once inside, I am able to stand by leaning against a wall.

After they feed me—a chicken thigh reheated for the occasion with a side of apple slices—I am treated to a series of questions not unlike those from my former interrogators.

"Could you tell me where you were approximately 10 years and 9 months ago?" the woman asks. She is sitting in a kitchen chair facing me while I wipe my mouth with the back of my hand. The boy sits on the floor at her feet, studying me.

I have fallen into the habit of evasion and so stall by asking her to repeat the question, which she does.

"If you could show me a newspaper for the day in question, it might help refresh my memory," I say.

"Of course," she says and opens an old trunk I hadn't noticed before, and after some shuffling of papers, presents a San Francisco newspaper for the very day she had inquired about.

"Checkmate," I say which enlists no reaction from the woman. The boy laughs.

"It's an important question to Bobby," the woman says.

I say I can barely remember yesterday let alone 11 years ago, though I will do my best. "Yesterday, to the best of my recollection, I was lying on a bed of thorns when a boy showed up..."

"That was me," Bobby says.

"And asked me if I was alive."

Two days ago or was it three, I was in unofficial custody at some nameless prison hospital.

Months before that, Molly was kidnapped with her consent by a posse of rogue government agents and taken to an unspecified island off the coast of Maine. Or so it was rumored.

Almost two years ago, I was a guest scholar at the Villa Mondare in northern Italy, reworking the first sentence of a new novel.

At some semi-distant point in the half-forgotten past—it could have been ten years ago—Molly announced that she was leaving me and was out the door before I could insist on an explanation.

When Molly left, I was vulnerable to the touch of air.

There were a succession of women in my life after that, some a product of my fantasies, perhaps all.

And years before that, Molly and I had what I think of as a shotgun wedding, the wounds from which still alive and complaining.

That's as much as I want to remember, and I ask the woman who calls herself Mina (short for Wilhemina) if I can have a few more days to sort things out.

The next morning—I spend the night on a hammock on the screened-in back porch—Bobby wakes me by slamming a door. When I open my eyes, trying to come to terms with where I am, he says, "Good morning, Papa."

Mina calls to Bobby from the next room, which may or may not be the kitchen. "Tell your father," she says, "that breakfast is being served."

How long have I been lost to myself? I knock at the door of memory and no one answers.

Is there something I've missed?

PART THREE

(Flight Dreams)

96th Night

I was, I fleetingly told myself, too old to run, but on the other hand not played out enough to stay. For days after I was more or less on my feet, my old (if older) self again, I was doing improvisatory rehearsals of my escape. Each morning, at the whisper of first light, I would take an extended walk from the house, varying direction in the continually thwarted hope of coming to some place I actually wanted to go, and then, not always easily, find my way back to what I thought of as a circumstantial domestic arrangement.

It was what they bargained for, wasn't it? They knew when they took me in, or should have known, that I had made a secondary career out of running away from seemingly comfortable situations. I had nothing against Mina and Bobby, but I had trouble imagining a scenario that included spending the rest of my life with them in a secluded cabin buried in the woods. The future I saw for myself was elsewhere.

Actually, I had no future in mind for myself. That is, I was open to a variety of futures and I didn't want to recapitulate the present routine indefinitely.

It was not in my scenario to be Bobby's father and Minna's prodigal husband returned.

Squeezed against her in her narrow bed, I would ask the uncommunicative Mina how and why she happened to live in an isolated cabin in the deep woods.

One time she said, "Oh this cabin has been in the family for at least a hundred years."

Another time, she said, "My mother gave me this place as a gift when Bobby was born."

Another time, she said, "Two guys from Denmark built it in the Danish fashion with imported logs to have a homelike home away from home. Things didn't work out as planned—one killed the other and fled no one seems to know where, leaving the house available for the first passerby, which was mother."

There were several other versions which contradicted in part some of the earlier versions. When she said, "Why do you think you have a right to know?" I decided to leave (setting gratitude and whatever aside) and not, not ever, come back.

The problem was, I hadn't to this point discovered a way out of the woods. I assumed—why wouldn't I?—that if I traveled long enough in any direction, I would eventually come to some outpost of civilization. Whatever there was.

Have I neglected to mention that there was a car on the premises, an ancient VW Beetle, which Mina would take off in periodically to bring in provisions? I never got to go with her, never found out where she went. Whenever Mina left the cabin for an extended period, it fell to me—it was my job by unspoken agreement—to babysit Bobby.

When I asked her how far it was to the nearest town, the answer I got was, "Far enough."

"How many miles exactly is far enough?" I asked, as if I didn't mind not knowing.

The only answer I ever got to that question was, "You don't want to know," said with a sassy smile.

I considered taking her ancient VW to make my escape, gave serious consideration to the idea about before rejecting it as unthinkable.

I could leave them in good conscience, but I couldn't take their transportation away from them.

I avoided sex with Mina the night before my planned escape so as not to deplete my limited energy.

I woke myself in the dark, tired as usual with a hard-on from sleeping pressed against Mina's ass, dressed in whatever came to hand, assuming as I started out—this my first go on the northern path—that first light was no more than an hour way.

I found myself taking small methodical steps in the dark, not wanting to lose the tricky path. Odd sounds emanated from the woods, but I had no idea, had not troubled to discover, what creatures might be out there.

I had a broomstick with me to use as a walking stick and as an emergency protection against the otherwise unforeseen.

As a precautionary measure, I swung my stick out in front of me like a blind man, driving off imaginary demons.

It seemed to be getting lighter, though it may only have been that my eyes had made private peace with the dark. It troubled me that the morning was so long in arriving. I worked myself into a frustrated rage at the night's protracted sway.

So I increased my pace, began to run, wanting to leave the night behind in my wake, aware as the path danced away and the brush swiped at me that it was a madman's hope.

Abruptly it was light and I reclaimed the path. It was a well-lit morning and I noticed a small black bear up ahead on its hind legs snatching berries from a bush. He was a few feet off the narrow path, too close to pass without calling attention to myself.

Impatience prodded me. Perhaps there was a way of getting by the bear, who was after all preoccupied with his breakfast, without his noting me.

I hunkered down, moved slowly ahead, tiptoed by him with apparent success, when a fallen branch snatched my ankle and I tripped noisily, grasping air. With a show of annoyance, the bear looked over in my direction—I pressed myself against a tree to avoid being seen—then after he had taken my measure (or had missed seeing me altogether), he returned to his task.

I hid behind the tree while considering what I might do to defend myself if the bear took it into his head to come after me.

And then the bear moved away, seemed to disappear briefly.

It was a while after I had passed his spot—I was still moving with extreme caution—perhaps a half-mile further along the path, when I heard footsteps behind. I quickened my pace at first but when the footsteps sounded behind me at the same or similar distance, I spun around to see who was there.

It was the same damn bear, tiptoeing on his hind legs, mimicking my pace in his deceptively quick lumbering manner. I fought back the impulse to run—surely he could have caught me if that was what he was up to—and continued warily at the pace I had set myself.

I knew very little about the habits of bears outside of folk lore and movies, though I had never heard of bears in any context trailing after people. I assumed that eventually—what could he possibly be thinking?—that he would discontinue his aberrant behavior.

But in fact what seemed like another hour passed and with it the five or six miles I had covered and the bear—I glanced back from time to time—was still the same relative distance behind me.

His idiot tenacity was getting on my nerves. He was on all fours when I turned around and I shook my fist at him and shouted at him to go away. I waved my arms at him to emphasize my point.

On his hind legs now, the bear gave the impression of waving back at me.

He seemed not to understand or at least was refusing to acknowledge that he did, shaking his head and looking abashed. Whatever was going on with him, he made no move to shorten the distance between us.

I took a few quick steps and then turned abruptly around to catch him off guard.

He was still approximately the same distance away. When he noticed that I was facing him, he did an almost graceful 360-degree turn.

Hard to explain what got into me, but the bear's antics amused me unreasonably—perhaps it was the release of tension—and I broke into a near-hysterical laugh, which he mimicked in his bearish way almost to perfection.

I decided not to be afraid of him—he had probably wandered off from a traveling circus—and I invited him, gesturing my intent, to join me. To my surprise, he refused and we continued walking in single file as we had before.

Weary of my long-running private dialogue, I tilted my head to the right and talked to the bear over my shoulder. I told him that after losing Molly, a loss that seemed to recapitulate itself, I had found it difficult to respond to other women. He acknowledged my lugubrious remarks with the occasional grunt.

Eventually we reached a clearing. Ahead in what seemed like a stage set for a town was a compound made up of institutional brick buildings. There was no immediate sign of life, but I thought I noticed a machine gun emplacement on the roof of one of the two-story buildings.

Though I had never seen the place from the outside before in daylight, I had no doubts as to where I was.

Clapping me on the shoulder as he went by, the bear scampered into the deserted clearing. I called to him to come back moments before a machine gun serenade welcomed him to the neighborhood.

I watched him lurch awkwardly into the woods, a howl of surprise preceding him. There was nothing I could do for him. Aggrieved at the loss of my companion, I veered off in the direction I had come, seeking other options.

97th Night

The world teetered on the brink of light when I woke. The others were already going about their morning routines, Bobby chopping firewood in the yard, Mina boiling water, wrestling with encroaching nature in the kitchen. I felt imprisoned in their routines.

I dressed in a black t-shirt and faded jeans, the clothes alongside the bed, and put on my old New Balance running shoes, which were showing signs of erosion.

I had a crust of bread with honey and a cup of herbal tea before announcing to Mina that I was going for a run. She said nothing, wore a ragged smile.

It was a partial lie for which I felt the barest whiff of guilt. I was going for a run, but I had, you see, no intention of returning.

I took the southern path this time, the one Mina had warned me against, noting that it could be dangerous while making a point of offering no particulars.

"How do you mean dangerous?" I asked.

Her answer was to roll her eyes.

"No, please," I said, "tell me what you mean. What's so dangerous about the southern path?"

"I've only heard rumors," she said. "It's the way things are, you know that. The world wherever you go, it's a dangerous place."

We kissed goodbye. I took Bobby's broomstick with me as protection against the unspeakable.

The sun came through the scrim of leaves, dappling the path making it all but impossible at times to see directly in front of me. When blinded by the sunlight, I tended to slow my pace until visibility returned.

Despite these periodic slowdowns, I felt I was making good time as if some kind of standard needed to be met. The only worry

I had was that I was not the least bit worried. I knew from a history of such experience that exhilaration carried with it promises of comeuppance.

Sometimes it seemed to me that during my periodic moments of blindness there had been something or someone there, haloed by the light, standing in my way, though when the glare passed whatever I had sensed was gone.

I put it down to a susceptibility to delusion perhaps set off by Mina's warning.

But this time when the sun receded there was clearly someone there, a smallish woman in a black dress, perhaps a nun's outfit, standing in the center of the path some ten feet away.

I was pleased to see another human being and I greeted her in a friendly manner and asked her where she had come from.

At first she said nothing, smiled nervously, then frowned. Then she mouthed the word "food," though it could just as easily been the word "fool."

I had some food and water with me in a ratty backpack, but hardly enough to satisfy my own burgeoning hunger. As a way of changing the subject, I asked her if she lived nearby. Perhaps she was actually some kind of nun and there was a monastery not far from here.

She smiled slyly, pointed again to her mouth, meaning whatever it meant, that she was hungry, had taken a vow of silence, was unable to speak.

I tore off a crust from the chunk of bread in my pack and held it out to the woman, who made no response.

"It's good bread," I said. "I assumed when you pointed to your mouth you were telling me you were hungry."

When I least expected it, she grabbed the crust from my hand and shoved it in her mouth.

In seconds, the crust, which she disposed of as if she were grinding mortar, was a memory and she pointed to her mouth again.

So I broke off another piece of bread and handed it to her

and then another after she obliterated the second piece with even greater dispatch than the first.

In short order, she had consumed the sizable chunk of bread I had been saving for my lunch but she seemed unsatisfied, pointing once again to her mouth, her gloved hand, which she held out toward me, trembling with expectation.

"That's all there is," I said, holding out empty hands.

"You've been so kind to an old woman," she seemed to say. "Still, I know there's more."

Reluctantly, I produced the hardboiled egg which had been nesting at the bottom of my pack, pretending to be surprised at its presence. She disposed of the egg without removing the shell.

And still she was unsatisfied, her hand pointing again to her mouth.

"I'm sorry," I said, shaking out the pack to show her there was no more food.

She picked up one of the books that had tumbled out and squeezed it into her mouth, disposing of it in three chomping bites.

The other, which was one of mine, she sniffed at, nibbled at the edges and then returned.

"Didn't we once dance together?" I asked her.

"That was my sister," she seemed to say.

Licking her lips, her tongue black with ink, she studied me for a protracted moment and then in apparent slow motion pirouetted. I didn't see her disappear. One moment she was there and the next she was gone.

I had a carrot in the pocket of my jeans, but I hesitated reaching for it. It seemed to move about restively as if it had a life of its own.

I had the path to myself again, but I hesitated moving on.

My first impulse after the hungry woman had disappeared was to return to Mina and Bobby, whom I suddenly missed or imagined I missed, abruptly aware of being alone in the world.

As a matter of will, I continued in the direction I had been going.

I made a point of shortening my stride so if I decided to return, which I promised myself was not going to happen, there would be a less demanding trip back.

I hadn't gotten much further when I arrived at the southern path's end, came to a crossroads in the woods. Having no basis for choosing right over left or left over right, I stood in place for the longest time, weighing the pros and cons of my next move, glancing one way then the other.

98th Night

"What do you think you're doing, honcho?" a voice called to me from behind a bush. "Didn't you see the signs? There's a dress rehearsal of a war going on at this site."

I had heard explosions in the distance, which I had attributed to thunder.

When the speaker in a major's uniform—his name tag read Grope—appeared from behind a bush, I recognized him (allowing for the alterations of aging) as my childhood friend, Lenny.

We had a brief reunion before returning to the business at hand.

"You better get out of here pronto, Honcho," he said, pulling me over to the side of the road—the bushes dense with troop life. "I'm under explicit orders to take no prisoners."

"Which way should I go?" I asked.

He thought about it, surveyed the scene in all directions.

"With all this random rocket action going on, there's no absolutely safe place to go. You may be best off hanging out in the bushes with the rest of us." At that moment, a missile exploded about twenty feet from the brush where the major's troops were hunkered down.

"Is that live ammo?" I asked.

"War is serious business, Honcho. You can't train one way and fight another. If you don't use live ammo, if you just go through the motions, the troops will think war is some kind of pussy picnic. You see what I'm saying. You got to practice the same way you play the real game. Don't worry about us—we're punishing the enemy shitloads more than he's punishing us."

I decided to go on. "Good to see you, " I said.

"Watch your ass," he said, hugging me while looking over my shoulder. "Believe me, the other side will not be as gentle with you if you get in their way."

I headed in a direction that with any luck would circumvent the troop activity of the other side.

A helicopter seemed to follow overhead and occasionally dumped what looked like sandwich wrappers in my direction. They were actually notes, warning me to move somewhere else unless I had no objection to being strafed in the next 10 minutes.

The notes offered no specific information as to the appropriate direction to go so I continued where I was heading though at a somewhat brisker pace.

At some point, a jeep cut me off and someone coming up behind me shouted "hostage," which is how I got taken prisoner by what I thought of at that point as the enemy.

I was frisked, blindfolded, my hands tied behind me, and dumped into the back of the jeep. "Where are you hiding your weapon?" someone asked.

"I'm a civilian," I protested.

"There are no civilians in war," another someone said, though it might have been the same voice.

I was briefly imprisoned in what smelled like a latrine—they let me out when someone of consequence insisted on coming in—then delivered me, my blindfold slipping over one eye, to what I assumed was the command tent.

The commanding officer, Colonel Field, looked on as his Adjutant interviewed me. Before the questions came, my blindfold was removed, my hands untied and I was offered my choice of coffee or tea.

I appreciated their kindness and asked if the coffee was fresh brewed before accepting the tea.

"We're the good guys," the Adjutant said, to which the Colonel nodded his approval, "but we're losing the war and we had to do something that we might otherwise disapprove of to increase our leverage. So by democratic vote among the senior officers, we decided to take a hostage from the other side to pressure them to release the officer class soldiers of ours they're holding prisoner as leverage against us. When our men saw you they knew right away from the way you were dressed—no ordinary person walks around in clothes as blatantly ratty as yours—that you were someone of consequence among the enemy. We hope that you'll be as frank with us and I have been with you. Who is it we have in our possession?"

"I'm a civilian," I said.

"The Colonel told me you would say exactly that," he said.

"I can understand your not wanting to betray your side, but what we're doing here is trying to end the bloodshed, not extend it. So by helping us, you would also be helping your friends. Our only goal is to establish a fair and lasting truce. Is that something you oppose?"

"Of course not," I said, "but..."

"I'm glad to hear that," he said. "You look like a civilized man. We're not asking for information on our enemy's troop movements, which you would be in your rights to deny us. All we want from you, in effect, is your name and rank."

I repeated my claim, told them that I had been walking in the woods and stumbled on their dress-rehearsal maneuver.

"So you say," the Adjutant said. "What if I told you that several of our men saw you embrace Major Grope, who is reputed to be second in command on the other side? Do you also want to deny that you embraced Major Grope?"

After that, I saw that there was nothing I could say to change their minds about me. "Look," I said, "you can tell Major Grope that you have his childhood friend, Honcho, in custody."

The Colonel and Adjutant shared knowing looks whose implications passed over my head. Before I was escorted from the command tent, the Adjutant thanked me for my cooperation and shook my hand.

For much of the next day, I was kept prisoner under armed guard in an adjoining tent.

I should mention that while this questioning was going on we were under almost continuous bombardment, most of the missiles exploding at a relatively safe distance.

I was using the latrine when a bomb fell just outside my box, shit flying about in the next few minutes as if it had wings.

When I let myself out—the door to the box had already fallen off—I discovered that my armed escort had been killed, half his head blown away. Also, the tent I had been staying in was a few flapping shreds of its former self.

Explosions lit up the sky and I saw through the trees perhaps a half mile away the gleam of paved roads. It may have been a mirage but I lowered my head (to make myself a smaller target) and ran a jagged path toward freedom. There was no point continuing in my role as useful hostage while the side that had captured me was being wiped out.

Along the way, I stumbled over what might have been the mangled body of the Adjutant—there was no time for mournful thoughts—as I hurried through the woods toward the paved roads of civilization.

99th Night

At long last, I was out of the woods, moving along the collar of a wide two-lane road with a snaky double line at its center. As a car neared, I would hold up my thumb half-heartedly in time-honored gesture. Repeated rejection soured my mood.

It was only after I decided not to raise my thumb that I got my first ride. It was from a middle-aged couple—a long married couple it seemed—in the throes of what might have been a twenty-year argument.

I didn't know how tired I was until the moment my rump met the back seat and I drifted off.

Even asleep, the voices of contention penetrated my cocoon and joined forces with whatever fragmentary dreams were playing on the same wave length.

"How far are you going?" the wife, who was in the driver's seat, asked whoever she thought she was talking to.

I might have answered but if I did it was with intention rather than speech. "As far as you're willing to take me," I might have said. I was in the business of creating distance between myself and the circumstantial domestic compromise I had taken pains to escape. When the game is escape, distance is the measure of accomplishment.

While accumulating distance, I felt oppressed by the ongoing dispute in the front seat that was my responsibility to resolve. They had chosen me as their audience and I had fallen asleep on the job. Couldn't I do anything right?

"When you can forgive yourselves," I said to their stand-ins in my dream, "you will be able to forgive each other." I was of course talking to myself.

"That's just the problem," the stand-in for the woman said. "He'll never forgive himself because he knows at the bottom of his soul that he's unforgivable."

"You know, sweetheart," the stand-in for the man said, "you can be a sanctimonious bitch. I suppose you're forgivable, right?"

"At least I can forgive myself," she said after an intake of breath, offering an icy laugh that sounded like glass breaking.

There was a moment, a measure, of silence and the car swerved to get out of its own way.

"Isn't one lane wide enough for you?" he said, addressing his remark to me.

"People with low self-esteem tend to be cruel to those closest to them," she said. "It's not his fault—he can't help himself."

"I won't dignify that with a reply," he said.

"You already have," she said.

"We need your help," the man said, nudging me with a rolled-up newspaper. "Are you awake?"

I blinked my eyes open and was disturbed to discover that we were parked at the side of the road. "What's going on?" I said.

"We need you to settle an argument," the man said. "You must have heard most of our argument. Tell us who you think is right."

"Right about what?" I asked.

They talked over each other in strident voices and what filtered through made little sense to me.

"Uh huh," I said, playing my part.

"We're not always like this," the woman said. "Zach needs an audience to express his..."

"Just shut up," he said, shouting her down. "Will you shut up, for God's sake."

At this point, the woman slapped her husband, a resounding blow, which he answered after a pregnant pause of outrage with a closed fist.

After he hit her in the eye, he apologized, but there were more blows to come, punctuated by apologies, curses and cries of pain.

Sensing they had forgotten me, I slipped out the door on my left and trotted off wearily in the direction the car was pointed. After awhile, my breath coming in echoes, assuming there was no immediate danger pursuing me, I slowed to a feverish stumble.

I was amazed how much the landscape I was passing resembled the landscape I had already passed.

It struck me as a profound discovery that the passing scene of the American road (if indeed this was America) tended to repeat itself as a kind of delayed emphasis. As I filed away this awareness for future use, a familiar lumbering car appeared alongside me, the passenger window rolled down.

"Please don't forsake us," the woman, who had an ugly bruise under her left eye, said. "We desperately need your help, Jack. We've agreed between us not to fight in your presence. We need someone of your seeming objectivity and wisdom to mediate our dispute."

"You've got the wrong person," I said. "I have no wisdom to offer."

"Nonsense," the woman said. "No matter. You have our word that we will defer to your wisdom whatever it is. Besides, Jack, this is not the direction you were escaping in when we picked you up."

She reached behind her and opened the back door.

I groaned silently, and with an unacknowledged sense of defeat, climbed into the skanky back seat, pulling the door shut behind me on the second try. The man, who was in the driver's seat, whisked the car around in a daring maneuver and we restarted our trip together as if for the first time.

100th Night

You're never out of the woods, I saw that now, even when you've planted your feet on paved roads. Unspecified time had passed— three days, a week, a month?—since I had kissed Mina and Bobby goodbye as prelude to taking a run through the woods from which I secretly hoped never to return. I had made a point of not thinking about them as I worked my way against unforeseen obstacles back to civilization.

The thing was, civilization as I remembered it, seemed to have disappeared while I was unavoidably elsewhere.

Days would pass with no signs of human habitation outside of two ratty gas station/convenience stores idling miles apart on opposite sides of the road.

Despite my single-minded pursuit of freedom, dumb luck had impeded my progress. The knowledge that I should have been further along at this point nagged at me with punishing regularity. I needed wheels to make time, but I had become with good reason wary of accessing another ride with strangers.

About a mile back, I had inquired of a clerk at the Puritan Farms self-service gas station as to where the nearest town was.

"This is the nearest town," she said.

"This?"

"We sell stamps in the back," she said. "We share a zip code with the Puritan Farms station on the other side of the road down aways. We think of ourselves as a town."

I asked her if she knew of a place in the area that rented cars.

She thought about my question for more time than I wanted to hang out in her store.

"There used to be one in the back of the middle school," she said, "but I don't think it did much business. I don't remember when it closed down—the owner died or something—but it was like ten years ago. Sorry."

As I walked along the side of the road, I kept glancing over my shoulder, expecting to see Mina's VW floating toward me in the distance. If I spotted her faded blue splotched with white Beetle before she spotted me, I could step back into the brush until it passed. I rehearsed the move periodically so as not to be taken by surprise.

After awhile, I came to what looked like a bus stop and I sat down on a rickety bench to await the next bus. I was awakened by a head sticking out the window of a sheriff's car that was idling a few feet from where I sat. "What's going on here?" the head asked.

"Isn't this a bus stop?"

He ignored my question. "You got any money?" he asked.

His question seemed presumptuous but I answered anyway so as not to give offense. "Some," I said. I also had a credit card but I didn't see the need to acknowledge all my assets on such short acquaintance.

"I'd also like to see some ID, if you don't mind," he said.

I did mind. "What's the problem?" I asked. No doubt my appearance had given him the wrong impression. My hands were grimy, there was a cut on my face, my pants had an alarming stain below the crotch.

"We have a nice town here," he said. "It's not that we don't like strangers, it's just that we like them better when they're somewhere else."

I got up from the bench and walked off into what was beginning to seem like a sunset. It passed my mind that he might shoot me in the back and I chose not to think about it.

When I looked up, the sheriff's car was crawling alongside me.

His twangy voice accosted me. "We were having this polite conversation when you jumped up and walked away," it said. "That's disrespect. Do you mean to be disrespectful?"

"I'm getting out of your town," I said.

"Is that right?" he said. "You might have told me so I could have arranged a parade. If there's no objection, I'll ride along to see that you don't get lost."

I didn't see that objecting would make a difference one way or another.

It felt odd walking alongside the sheriff's car, which was mimicking my pace, but it must have felt odd from his vantage also. At some point, he offered me a ride since, as he put it, we were both going in the same direction.

I said I didn't mind walking, but five minutes later he asked again.

I noted, though there hadn't been much traffic, that a string of cars was piling up behind him.

"You don't get anywhere being a hard-head," he said. "I know how lonely it can be being out on the road by yourself. And you must be tired. You're not so young any more."

With measured reluctance, I accepted his third offer of a ride. I didn't trust him but I had the sense that one of the cars in the group crawling behind us—the fourth or fifth— was Mina's ancient faded-blue Beetle and this at the moment seemed the lesser of two unpleasant alternatives.

Sheriff Mike, as he called himself, didn't seem so bad up close, though there was the musty odor about him of someone who hadn't bathed in a while. It may have been me I was inhaling or the inside of the car, but it came to the same thing.

Anyway, the sheriff wanted to talk and it seemed not to matter a lot who was the one on the other end. "You ever been married?" he asked but he went on as if my answer, if offered, would have made little difference. "I been married twenty-three years to the same woman before she left me for some damn salesman who was passing through. When she was gone, even though I kind of missed having her around, it struck me that I never loved her. That's a terrible thing to realize.

And what was worse, and much worse, I couldn't remember if there was anyone I ever loved. Which has to mean there wasn't ever anyone. Not anyone fucking ever. At the same time, I could remember the names of seven people I flat out hated. What does that say about my life? Then I began to wonder if anyone ever loved anyone. You know what I mean?"

While I was thinking about his question, the sheriff went on to another subject. "You ever kill anybody?" he asked, glancing at me to see my reaction. "When I first took this job—believe it or not I wasn't always a sheriff—I hadn't had much experience with killing my own species. You could probably count the number on one three-fingered hand. Of course there isn't much opportunity to kill in a small burg like this. In most cases, a good sound beating would serve the same purpose." He paused for breath.

I had lost the train of his thought. "What purpose is that?" I asked.

He stepped on the brake abruptly and we stopped with a jolt. My head bruised the windshield. The horn of the car behind made a mild almost-unintelligible protest. Meanwhile, we were moving again. We passed a diner that had been boarded up, what looked like the remains of a For Sale sign lying like a sacrifice to some heathen deity at the foot of the front door. Next to the diner was a furniture store long since deserted, a Sale sign in the dark window with a spidery crack separating the "a" and the "l."

This is where my jurisdiction ends," he said, pulling into the dirt lot behind the furniture store.

"Where are we?" I asked.

"This is where you get out," he said, turning off the ignition. He waited for me to climb out the door before he eased himself out from the driver's side.

Looking to make amends, I thanked him for the ride, taking a few backwards steps. "Wherever we are," I said, "I guess I'm a little closer to where I'm going than I would have been had I walked."

The sheriff came around the car in my direction.

"Thanks again," I said, making a move to turn away while still keeping him in sight.

He kept his hands at his sides much like a gunfighter waiting for whoever dared to make the first move. "I'm going to ask you to run," he said.

When you suspect that your life is on the line, your senses become increasingly acute. I noticed a rock the size of a child's baseball a few feet away and I contrived to stumble and fall on top of what I perceived to be a possible weapon.

When I was standing again still facing the sheriff who hadn't moved, I had the rock in my hand. "I'm going," I said, taking another step backwards. There was no one around, though I heard an unseen car grinding along in the near distance. I showed him my back for a moment, but desperate curiosity got the better of me and I turned again to face him.

All I can say in my defense was that he was drawing his gun, that it had already cleared his holster when I hurled the rock with an abrupt sidearm motion, catching him above the left eye. I may have heard the gun fire, the indistinct sound echoing. It may even have fired twice as he made up his mind to fall.

The big man fell like timber, a hand in the air as if brushing something unseen away, and that's when I began to run.

At that moment, a faded blue VW huffed its way up the dirt road in seeming slow motion, kicking up gravel. I recognized the woman driving and the boy, somewhat older than I remembered him, dozing in the back seat. I got in without hesitation and momentarily we were on the road.

It was possible, wasn't it, that the sheriff only meant to frighten me? I forgave myself, or tried to, for being unforgivable.

I may have heard an ominous siren in the distance or I may only have imagined the official music of police pursuit, but for the moment there was no car in the rearview mirror coming up behind us. In gratitude or perhaps love, I brushed Mina's shoulder with the back of my hand,

"How long it's taken you to find us," she said.

101st Night

When I claimed consciousness this morning, I was fifteen-years-old—yesterday had been my birthday—and I was lying in bed with a woman almost old enough to be my mother. Though she was lying on her side facing away, I could tell from the hair color and body style that she was not my actual mother. I couldn't remember whether we had a sexual history together or not.

The odd thing was, I knew what was awaiting me, remembered in thinly veiled outline the essential details of the next forty-five years of my life. At first, it seemed like an advantage, thinking I might avoid this time around some of the misjudgments I was destined to make.

If you had nothing new to look forward to, it hardly seemed worth the effort to echo an already-failed past. One of the pleasures of life was the exhilaration of surprise.

I got out of bed and collected my clothes from virtually every corner of the room. It struck me that the older woman still asleep in my bed had been a birthday gift from my father, who had been announcing everywhere (I always assumed it was a joke) that it was about time I lost my virginity.

Perhaps nothing much had happened between us because I knew for a fact that my main stage sexual debut was several months down the road and that in fact I lost my virginity to Lenny's sexy older sister, Sybil. It was possible, I suppose, to have forgotten my one-night stand with this older woman hiding her face in my childhood bed and that sexy Sybil was actually my second between the legs.

After Sybil, until I met (and married) Hannah, I pursued a few women here and there (really girls) whose names escape me, with limited success. What do I mean by limited success? I mean everything more or less but the one thing that counted (at fifteen) on your permanent reputation. What these unremembered members of the opposite sex had in common was that each in her own way had denied me what I assumed I needed. And so I married Hannah, who denied me nothing. And once we were married—the reasons, there always reasons—our sexual life was reduced to talking about what we no longer allowed ourselves to do. And then, one day, without advance word, Hannah went home to her mother to resume her interrupted childhood.

That shouldn't have happened.

The detritus of that loss never went away not even after I married Anna and passed in the world as an adult. Not even after I behaved badly, choosing desire over obligation, and ran off with Molly. Not even after the memorable early years with Molly when we were mostly almost happy. When Molly left to find her uncharted real self, it was as if Hannah were leaving me all over again.

But at this moment I was just one day past fifteen and all of my failed relationships were still out there in the murky distance of future time.

"Did we?" I asked the woman, who showed some signs of stirring.

It was odd that I could remember the major events of what hadn't happened yet but no telling details from the recent past.

"What time is it?" she asked. "I must have fallen asleep. I never intended to stay the night."

When she emerged from the bed—I had my back turned so as not to reveal the extent of my vain unappeasable need—she was fully dressed. "Do my parents know you're here?"

"You told me they were away," she said.

Did I? They almost never went anywhere—my father liked to sleep in his own bed—so it was hard to imagine where they might be if not somewhere in the house. "Did I mention when they'd be back?" I asked.

"It doesn't matter, sweetheart," she said, caressing my face. "I'll be on my way."

I searched the files of memory for her name and the only thing that came to mind was Mrs. Andsons, who was the local pharmacist's wife. I spoke it under my breath so she could avoid responding if it wasn't her own.

"Yes?" she said.

I had no question for her or none I felt comfortable asking, but I couldn't let this opportunity pass unventured without losing respect for myself. "You might think this is a weird thing to ask," I said, "but I must have had too much to drink because I don't remember what we did last night. What did we... do?"

"You have nothing to reproach yourself with," she said, "nothing."

If she intended her comment to ease my mind, it served in fact to exacerbate my uneasiness. "Nothing?" I asked.

"Nothing," she said. "You'll have to excuse me now, Jack. I really have to get home and make nice. When I'm not in the old tyrant's bed overnight, he's subject to evil thoughts in the morning."

I tried to think of something to say that would keep her with me a little longer but nothing I came up with sounded quite right. At the last, I made the worst of several possible choices. "Give me another chance," I said.

She took a step toward me which she instantly nullified by taking a step back. "Sweetheart, I can't," she said. "It's so sweet of you to ask and I am tempted, but no, no I can't. Maybe another time. You never know. The gift-wrapped package of Trojans I brought over, darling, are in the sock drawer of your dresser."

She blew me a kiss and escaped through a series of doors into the street and I watched her ruefully from the window. She seemed to morph into Molly as she hurried away.

Even in my dreams, even with a willing partner, I couldn't get it right.

I went back to bed and closed my eyes with renewed resolution.

This time when Hannah and I made love for the first time, it would not be in the backseat of my father's Dodge.

This time I would not have sex with Anna's friend, Yvonne, in an airport phone booth.

This time I would not disappoint Molly, betray Anna, run from Mina. I would continue to love them no matter how badly we treated each other. If you refuse to acknowledge disillusion, love can survive anything.

No matter, I would wake in the morning an old man in Mina's bed.

Nevertheless at fifteen years and a day, setting hypocrisy aside, all I really wanted in this life— the be-all and end-all of my childhood aspirations—was to get my ashes hauled, get laid, get screwed, get fucked, get going.